Titles by MaryJanice Davidson

UNDEAD AND UNWED
UNDEAD AND UNEMPLOYED
UNDEAD AND UNAPPRECIATED
UNDEAD AND UNRETURNABLE
UNDEAD AND UNPOPULAR
UNDEAD AND UNEASY
UNDEAD AND UNWORTHY
UNDEAD AND UNWELCOME
UNDEAD AND UNFINISHED
UNDEAD AND UNDERMINED
UNDEAD AND UNSTABLE

DERIK'S BANE
WOLF AT THE DOOR

SLEEPING WITH THE FISHES
SWIMMING WITHOUT A NET
FISH OUT OF WATER

Titles by MaryJanice Davidson and Anthony Alongi

JENNIFER SCALES AND THE ANCIENT FURNACE
JENNIFER SCALES AND THE MESSENGER OF LIGHT
THE SILVER MOON ELM: A JENNIFER SCALES NOVEL
SERAPH OF SORROW: A JENNIFER SCALES NOVEL
RISE OF THE POISON MOON: A JENNIFER SCALES NOVEL
EVANGELINA: A JENNIFER SCALES NOVEL

Anthologies

CRAVINGS

(with Laurell K. Hamilton, Rebecca York, Eileen Wilks)

BITE

(with Laurell K. Hamilton, Charlaine Harris, Angela Knight, Vickie Taylor)

KICK ASS

(with Maggie Shayne, Angela Knight, Jacey Ford)

MEN AT WORK

(with Janelle Denison, Nina Bangs)

DEAD AND LOVING IT

SURF'S UP

(with Janelle Denison, Nina Bangs)

MYSTERIA

(with P. C. Cast, Gena Showalter, Susan Grant)

OVER THE MOON

(with Angela Knight, Virginia Kantra, Sunny)

DEMON'S DELIGHT

(with Emma Holly, Vickie Taylor, Catherine Spangler)

DEAD OVER HEELS

MYSTERIA LANE

(with P. C. Cast, Gena Showalter, Susan Grant)

MYSTERIA NIGHTS

(includes Mysteria *and* Mysteria Lane, *with P. C. Cast, Susan Grant, Gena Showalter)*

UNDERWATER LOVE

(includes Sleeping with the Fishes, Swimming Without a Net, *and* Fish out of Water*)*

DYING FOR YOU

Dying
for You

MaryJanice Davidson

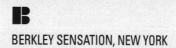

BERKLEY SENSATION, NEW YORK

THE BERKLEY PUBLISHING GROUP
Published by the Penguin Group
Penguin Group (USA) Inc.
375 Hudson Street, New York, New York 10014, USA
Penguin Group (Canada), 90 Eglinton Avenue East, Suite 700, Toronto, Ontario M4P 2Y3, Canada
(a division of Pearson Penguin Canada Inc.) • Penguin Books Ltd., 80 Strand, London WC2R 0RL,
England • Penguin Group Ireland, 25 St. Stephen's Green, Dublin 2, Ireland (a division of Penguin
Books Ltd.) • Penguin Group (Australia), 250 Camberwell Road, Camberwell, Victoria 3124, Australia
(a division of Pearson Australia Group Pty. Ltd.) • Penguin Books India Pvt. Ltd., 11 Community
Centre, Panchsheel Park, New Delhi—110 017, India • Penguin Group (NZ), 67 Apollo Drive,
Rosedale, Auckland 0632, New Zealand (a division of Pearson New Zealand Ltd.) • Penguin Books
(South Africa) (Pty.) Ltd., 24 Sturdee Avenue, Rosebank, Johannesburg 2196, South Africa

Penguin Books Ltd., Registered Offices: 80 Strand, London WC2R 0RL, England

This is a work of fiction. Names, characters, places, and incidents either are the product of the author's
imagination or are used fictitiously, and any resemblance to actual persons, living or dead, business
establishments, events, or locales is entirely coincidental. The publisher does not have any control over
and does not assume any responsibility for author or third-party websites or their content.

"The Fixer-Upper" copyright © 2004 by MaryJanice Davidson Alongi. Previously published in *Men at Work*.
"Paradise Bossed" copyright © 2006 by MaryJanice Alongi. Previously published in *Surf's Up*.
"Driftwood" copyright © 2007 by MaryJanice Alongi. Previously published in *Over the Moon*.
"Witch Way" copyright © 2007 by MaryJanice Alongi. Previously published in *Demon's Delight*.
Cover illustration John Jay Cabuey.
Cover design Leslie Worrell.
Interior text design by Kristin del Rosario.

PUBLISHING HISTORY
Berkley Sensation trade paperback edition / August 2012

Library of Congress Cataloging-in-Publication Data

Davidson, MaryJanice.
Dying for you / MaryJanice Davidson.—Berkley Sensation trade pbk ed.
p.   cm.
ISBN 978-0-425-24678-8 (pbk.)
I. Title.
PS3604.A949D95   2012
813'.6—dc23   2012020130

PRINTED IN THE UNITED STATES OF AMERICA

10 9 8 7 6 5 4 3 2 1

CONTENTS

The Fixer-Upper

For Stacy,
who gave me the idea

ACKNOWLEDGMENTS

Thanks as always to my family for their support. And especially to my sister, who never minds when I cancel our plans so I can finish a story.

AUTHOR'S NOTE

There are no such things as ghosts, which only means that I have never seen one.

Prologue

He dodged, laughing, and lost his footing. The fun stopped as the stairs rushed up at him. Adrenaline was dumped into his system, but there was nothing to clutch onto, nothing to slow his fall. The last thing he heard, besides his neck breaking between the third and fourth vertebrae, was his sister, screaming.

He did plenty of screaming himself, but no one could hear him, and no one could see him.

He stayed gone for a long time.

Chapter 1

"And if you would sign here . . . and initial here . . . and sign here . . . and here again . . ."

Cathy signed and initialed until her hand cramped. Catherine Sarah Wyth. CSW. Thank goodness for all those little red Sign Here notes, or she would have been lost. Even *with* her realtor.

"And here's a check."

"What a pleasant surprise," she said, and she meant it. The house she was buying was already draining money; it was nice that they'd overestimated closing costs. She could buy a new couch! Well, half a couch. A cushion, maybe. "Is that it? Are we done?"

Her realtor, John Barnes, looked across the table at the owner's lawyer, John Barney. Like *that* never got confusing. "I think we're okay, here, how about you, John?"

"Fine, John. Cathy." John #1 stood to shake her hand. "I hope you'll be very happy in your new house. I have to say it's nice that something positive could come out of tragedy."

"Thanks, John," she replied, barely listening—she was too busy mentally redecorating her new fixer-upper. Then she shook hands with John #2. "John." She scooped up the folder with roughly 1,212 pieces of paperwork, and carefully tucked her check in her purse. "Okay, well, I guess I'll go check out the house."

My new house.

"Congratulations," John #2 said.

"Good luck," John #1 said.

"Thank you, gentlemen. Have a good one." She skipped out the doorway, remembered herself, then said to hell with it and skipped the rest of the way to her car. The last time she had skipped to anything she had had a consuming interest in Super Balls and Lik 'Em Aid. She still liked Lik 'Em Aid, but everything else had changed.

She drove straight to 1001 Tyler Avenue in St. Paul, Minnesota, parked in *her* driveway, and stared up at *her* house.

Her house.

Even now, she couldn't believe it was real. All those years of saving, of making a pair of shoes last two years and a suit last four, of going without nice vacations and pricey clothes and fancy cars, lobster tails and caviar—not that she could abide fish eggs, but still—had finally paid off. She was a home owner.

She climbed out of her car—yet another sacrifice to her

new home; it was a 1994 Ford Taurus and it wheezed in the cold—and stood in her yard, then strolled around the—her—property.

The turrets, in particular, delighted her. Like something Rapunzel would hang out in. And the mini-porch up on the roof. The bay windows, the huge kitchen—it seemed especially huge after years of apartment efficiencies.

It definitely needed work. For one thing, the house wasn't really pink . . . over the years, the deep red had faded. It had probably looked a lot nicer in 1897. The porch steps looked downright dangerous—a lawsuit waiting to happen—and the fence looked like broken teeth. The garden had been, to put it politely, overrun.

It wasn't surprising—the woman who had sold the house to Cathy had been, at rough guess, a thousand years old. Not that she had seen the woman, but Cathy knew she was an original descendent of the family who had built the home. Spry she was not. The house had, understandably, eventually been too much for her.

That was all right. That was, in fact, the only reason Cathy had been able to afford a 2,800-square-foot home at her age, on her salary. And she had wanted this place the moment she saw it on the Edina Realty website. Not because it was big, although that was nice. But because it was a home. It had character. And if it needed work, well, Cathy had never been afraid to get her hands dirty.

She heard a pounding and looked over to the yard on her left. A shirtless fellow had his back to her, had something set up on those whatchamacall'ems—the things you set something on when you were going to hammer them. Or something. Horses? No, that couldn't be right.

Anyway, the guy was really pounding away, and sweat was gleaming across his broad back. It was only May, but Cathy felt herself start to sweat in response. Oofta. Broad back, narrow waist, tool belt, faded jeans. It was like watching a Bowflex commercial.

He turned, still holding the hammer, and their gazes met across the low hedge. How romantic. She could see how dark his eyes were from all the way across her yard. Gorgeous brown eyes, full mouth, aquiline nose. Strong chin, long neck, broad yummy shoulders. His chest was lightly furred, the hair tapering down to a line leading straight to his, um, belt. He looked like a moody prince, out to do a little carpentry work before running the country.

New house. No more renting. A decent temp job. A yummy next-door neighbor. Oh, lucky, lucky day!

"Well, fuckin' A," her prince said. "A new neighbor. Fuckin' great! Hey, how the fuck are ya?"

Oh dear, she thought.

Chapter 2

"So you're a temp worker, huh? Like a new job every week?"

"Something like that." She topped off her neighbor's water glass. Well, water Dixie cup.

"Can't hold a job, huh?" He guffawed, throwing his long neck back. She smiled thinly and said nothing. The truth was, she hated to be tied down. Trying a new job every month or so suited her perfectly. "Well, that's a bitch."

"Not really. I'm sorry, I didn't get your name . . . ?"

"Ken Allen."

"I'm Cathy."

"Aww, Ken and Cathy, that's kinda cute."

"Not really. Well, I've got a lot of work to do . . ."

"I'll help you move in," he said immediately. She noticed it wasn't a question.

"That's okay. You're busy, and my friends are coming over tomorrow to—"

"You gotta have some stuff with you. Chicks always bring shit with them."

"As a matter of fact, I do have some shit with me, but you don't have to—"

He ignored her, got up, and moved toward the kitchen door. "I'll go get it."

She trailed after him, uncomfortable and silent. The truth was, she never knew how to behave around strong-willed—okay, obnoxious—people. She herself was more the quiet type. Her best friend was strong-willed enough for the both of them. Give her a book and a cup of tea and she was in heaven. She tended to stay out of the way of such people. Then she'd spend days despising herself for her cowardice, but she was definitely a low-road kind of girl, and that was all there was to it.

"What a piece of shit," he said upon seeing her car.

"Thank you," she replied neutrally.

"Friend of mine owns a Chevy dealership. I'll get you set up."

"Thanks, but that's really not—"

"I'll call him for you tomorrow."

"Thanks, but frankly, after buying a new house, the last thing I need to do is—"

"Go pop the trunk."

Grinding her teeth, she did so. He's just being nice, she told herself. A good neighbor.

"Gotta tell you," he said, lugging her boxes and suitcases

inside with zero strain—ooh, those rippling muscles "it's nice to have that fucking old bitch out of here."

"That's so sweet." She'd never met someone so equally handsome and obnoxious. The foul words that kept coming out of that sinfully sullen mouth nearly made her gasp. "And by sweet, I mean vaguely disturbing."

"What?"

"Nothing."

"Nice to have somebody you can look at, you know? You know, you'd be almost cute if you cut your hair and didn't button your shirt all the way up."

"Okay. Well, thanks," she said as he set down the last of the boxes in her living room. "I'm sure you want to get back to your project."

"Fuckin' A. I'll see you around, Cathy."

Why did that sound like a threat? She shrugged it off as single-woman paranoia and set about emptying the few boxes she had brought for Closing Day.

Chapter 3

"Oh my God!" her best friend and worst enemy, Nikki, gasped and nearly swooned. "Who is *that?*"

"My next door neighbor. You'd like him; he's vulgar."

"Don't tease." Nikki lasciviously wiggled her eyebrows. "Day-amn! Cute, cute, *cute!*"

"Knock yourself out." Then, louder as Ken approached, she said, "Good morning."

"Hey." He nodded to Nikki. "Hey."

"Nikki, this is my next door neighbor, Ken Allen. Ken, this is my best friend, Nikki Sheridan."

"Hey," he repeated.

"Well, hi there. Nice to meet you."

"Do you *own* a shirt?" Cathy asked politely. Shirtless Ken

was once again flawlessly, if casually, attired in work boots, jeans, and a tool belt.

"It's too fuckin' hot," he complained. "You're lucky I'm even helping you move all your shit."

"So, so lucky," she replied, annoyed at the amused look on Nikki's face. They had known each other since the fourth grade and were more like sisters than friends—like a close family member, she often wanted to strangle Nikki, or at least banish her. The flip side was, if anyone ever threatened Nikki, Cathy would take a baseball bat to their frontal lobe. "Thank you for coming over."

"Yeah." He turned his back to them and trotted down the porch steps, sidestepping her other friends and wrestling the television out of the back of the rental van.

"I said it before and I'll say it again: day-amn!"

"He's obnoxious," Cathy muttered under her breath.

"Like you could do so much better. If you could, sunshine, you would have by now."

"Here comes the 'you're not getting any younger' speech."

"Well, you're not. You're on the wrong side of your twenties, girlfriend, and you've got a golden opportunity right next door."

"He's not what I would call golden," she commented.

"Golden tan," Nikki said dreamily. "God, he must work out ten hours a day. In the sun. Getting sweaty. All sweaty in the blazing sun. Ummm . . ."

"Go for it. You two were made for each other."

"Meaning I'm an obnoxious bitch," she said cheerfully,

taking no offense. "Thanks tons. Hey, he wouldn't be coming over here if he didn't think you were cute."

"I'm not cute," she said coldly. "Kittens are cute. I'm a grown woman."

"Says the five-foot-nothing shrimp-o," Nikki said, smugly secure with her five feet, ten inches. "You've got to get over the cute thing. It's not a dirty word, y'know. You're short, you're gorgeous, women pay hundreds of dollars to make their hair as curly—"

"Frizzy."

"—as yours is naturally, and you've got Sinatra blue eyes. You're like a gypsy princess with Sinatra eyes."

"Why, Nikki. That was almost poetic." Nikki always saw her friends as gorgeous beauties, which sounded like a good quality, but really was a little on the annoying side. Particularly if you were the type who knew you weren't beautiful. "I didn't know you cared."

Nikki ignored the jibe. "Now you're getting pissy because he's attracted to you?"

"He doesn't know me."

"Hardly anybody does, sugarplum. You're kind of famous for keeping us all at arm's length."

"It certainly doesn't work on you."

"No chance, baby," she said, grinning. "I know I'm your hero."

"I suspect Ken's interest in me is strictly of the novelty type."

"It's what what of the what?"

"I'm here," she explained, "like Everest. So he's interested."

"So? That's as good a reason as any to get sweaty with a sexy neighbor."

"Nikki . . ."

"Come on, let's get you moved in."

Nikki was right, Cathy thought, following her friend to the van. *She is my hero. I could never be so relaxed, so fun. So obnoxious and blunt. But I'm not going for Ken, no matter how much she nags me. It just wasn't meant to be.*

However, I have no plans to buy him a shirt in the near future.

Chapter 2

She couldn't find her keys, which was infuriating and, worse, made her want to cry with frustration. She hated, *hated* not being able to find things. It's why she was still unpacking at 3:00 A.M. It's why she decided it was a good time to drive to the local 24-hour supermarket and stock the fridge, so when she got up in the morning—later today, rather—she could have her toast and yogurt and tea.

"Goddammit!" she cried, running her fingers through her frizz—yes, that's right, *frizz*, never mind how often Nikki admired her hair and said it was curly and, ugh, cute. "Where are you?"

She had a place for them, of course—the drawer in the writing desk in her foyer. That was where they belonged. That was where they *should* be. But she'd lent them to Karl so he could move her car out of the way of the van, and who knew where he'd put them? Karl was an engineer, so you'd think he was reliable, but the fact was, he was infamous for losing his checkbook, his keys, his contact lens case. What had she been thinking, letting him take her keys?

She'd looked everywhere. Everywhere. If she didn't find them soon, she was calling Karl, and never mind how late it was. He was probably up, anyway, playing another marathon session of War Craft.

She started going through the kitchen drawers again, which was stupid because she *knew* they weren't there. Then, oddly, she heard a familiar jingle. She turned . . . and froze in place as her keys bumped down the back stairs and slid across the floor, stopping two inches from her left big toe.

She was tired.

She was tired, and it had been a long day—a day not over yet—and she was very, very tired. And, apparently, the proud new owner of a haunted house.

"No I'm not," she said aloud. "I'm just tired. They were probably there all the time and I-I made a little mind movie to explain how they got there."

The keys, resting beside her foot, suddenly raised themselves up two inches and shook, jangling merrily.

She ran out the back door, but not before she bent and scooped them up.

"Ken! Ken, let me in!" She hammered on the door until her fist went numb. "Ken, I've got to come in!"

He opened the door and blinked at her, swaying slightly.

She could smell the beer before he even opened his mouth. "Say, Cathy, hey-hey. Whatchoo doing here?"

She bulled past him and stood in his kitchen, wrapping her arms around herself for comfort. "I—something weird happened and—I'm sorry to bother you so late. It's just I don't know anybody in the neighborhood except you and I-I didn't know what to do."

"Thass okay." He was shirtless, and pantless, splendidly arrayed in navy blue boxers. No tool belt this time. His hairy legs, she wasn't too rattled to note, were long, lean, and smoothly muscled. "M'glad you came over." He lurched toward her and clumsily pawed for her breasts, but due to his extreme inebriation, and her extreme shortness, he groped her shoulders instead. "Less go upstairs? Hmmm?"

"On second thought," she said, removing his hand, "I will take my chances with the ghost. Good night." She managed to evade his drunken gropings and soon found herself back in her house. Her haunted house.

"Okay," she said out loud. "Let's think about this." Going to Ken had been a stupid mistake—a stupid, hysterical, childish mistake. For God's sake. She was a grown woman and what had she done? Run away like a coward and shaken like a puppy in a stranger's kitchen, a stranger she was beginning to really dislike. Because her keys had moved by themselves. Stupid, stupid!

"It wasn't necessarily a bad thing," she continued aloud. "The keys showed up, right?"

A definitive rap, as if unseen knuckles had knocked on the ceiling.

"Okay," she said again, taking a deep, steadying breath. "Are you one of my friends playing a joke? I promise I won't get mad."

Two raps.

"This was your house?"

One rap.

"Well, it's . . . it's my house now," she said with a firmness she most definitely did not feel. "I mean to say, I will be living here from now on. I-I hope that's all right."

One rap.

"Good. My name is Cathy. If one rap equals A, and two raps equal B, and three equals C, and so forth, what is your name?"

J-A-C-K.

"Well, it's . . . it's nice to meet you," she said, feeling foolish. Part of her could hardly believe this was happening. It *had* to be a joke. Because otherwise, her beloved pink Victorian was haunted, and did she really want to share living space with the dead?

No. She did not.

"I'm . . . I'm going out now. To get groceries. Will you be here when I get back?"

Nothing.

"Hello?"

Nothing.

Feeling both disappointed and relieved, Cathy managed to walk, not run, out of the house this time.

Chapter 5

No one named Jack had ever lived in her house.

Cathy had spent her lunch break doing extensive research and web surfing into land, deeds, home ownership, and spirits. She quickly determined her ghost was not a poltergeist, and did not seem malevolent, but she had less luck finding out who it—he—was. But apparently, his silence after the evening's excitement was not atypical: manifesting seemed to really tire out a ghost.

The question was: did she mind?

She did not know; it was too early to tell. All it—he—had done was talk to her and produce her keys. Then nothing for the rest of the night, or the entire next day—Sunday—or this morning.

She couldn't discuss this with Nikki, because her friend had a strong streak of practicality. If she couldn't see it or touch it, it wasn't real. Cathy, however, tended to believe her senses. Her keys moved by themselves. Someone had spelled out the letters J, A, C, and K. If it wasn't a practical joke, which she had not entirely ruled out—though if it *was* a joke, no one had come forward and it was going on too long—then she was prepared to believe her house was haunted. It was certainly old enough to house a spirit or two.

She thought about calling her real-estate agent, John #1, then immediately decided against it. She'd been living in her new house less than seventy-two hours. It was a little early to go running for help.

And whatever would she tell him? "Hello, John, the house you sold me is haunted and I . . . I . . ." What? Wanted a refund? Not hardly. She wasn't going back to pouring money down the rent rathole. Not ever. She had felt like a drone bee in a hive, living in those low-personality apartment complexes.

She decided to go about her business as usual, and see what the ghost—if it *was* a ghost—did next.

"Perfect," she said as lightning crashed outside her window. It was a dark and stormy night. No, really. "That's just perfect."

She had finished the unpacking and was almost swaying with exhaustion. But it was finished, all finished. A place for everything and she had put everything in its place. Now the house felt a little more like her house.

A little. She still couldn't believe it when she pulled into the driveway and realized this was her house. She owned it and lived there and it was hers. She supposed the feeling of euphoric surprise would go away someday. It was almost a shame.

The storm had started about three hours ago, and was building up to a rare fury—rare for St. Paul, anyway. As long as it wasn't a blizzard, most Minnesotans didn't get too annoyed by the weather. That might change, today, especially if—

The lights went out.

"And again," she said aloud. "Perfect." Rats and double rats. Where had she unpacked candles? After a moment's thought, she remembered they were in one of the kitchen drawers, as were the—

"One more time," she said as she heard a kitchen drawer open by itself, heard things clink and shift around, heard a candle rolling in the dark toward her. "Perfect."

She looked down and, when lightning flashed again, saw two candles bump up against her foot, along with a small box of matches she'd grabbed the last time she'd had sushi at Kikugawa.

"Thank you," she said. Testing, she added, "Thank you, Jack."

No response.

She bent, picked up a candle, lit it, used the lit candle to light the other one, stood. She still had a very real sense of unreality about the whole business, but one thing was certain: having a ghost around could be handy.

Chapter 6

Her weekly duty was almost completed. Ah, to be so close to the end, and yet have it remain so tantalizingly out of reach.

"Cathy? You still there?"

"Still here, Dad," she confirmed. Her father lived in Missouri with her Wicked Stepmother, or W for short.

Not that there was a thing wrong with Kitty Wyth (if one overlooked the absurdity of referring to a fifty-eight-year-old woman as "Kitty," which was difficult even during the best of times).

Cathy had lost her mother to breast cancer when she herself was barely into puberty—possibly the worst time to lose a parent. And she was not prepared to welcome anyone who was there to take her mother's place. Thus, Kitty had been dubbed W and that was it, that was all there was to it. She was Wicked, sleeping in Cathy's mother's bed. She was

The Stepmother—not the true Mrs. Wyth—and that was the end of it.

"Maybe Kitty and I should come up to see you. Maybe Labor Day Weekend," her father suggested doubtfully. Warm family get-togethers were not their thing. This was, Cathy knew, entirely her fault. W had done nothing wrong; had tried, many many times, to make Cathy feel included and loved.

If she could not have her mother's love, Cathy did not want the love of a grown woman named Kitty.

This, she knew, made her a bad person.

"Well," she replied, not actually answering her father, "it was nice talking to you."

"Yeah. You, too." He hung up. Her father never said good-bye.

She walked into the kitchen to hang up the phone and saw one of her mother's china plates on the table, with one of the frosted sugar cookies she'd picked up at the bakery that morning. Beside the plate was a small glass of milk.

"Right, Jack. Because I need that on my thighs," she joked.

"Who are you talking to?"

Cathy turned and saw Nikki standing in front of her screen door. "Myself," she replied easily. She ignored Jack's indignant knock and let Nikki in. "Oh, good, you've started dropping in without calling first. I was afraid you wouldn't pick up any bad habits this year."

"Go fuck yourself," her friend replied cheerfully. "I was in the neighborhood—that bakery is kick ass—and thought I'd come over." She held up a white wax paper bag and shook it.

"Oh no," Cathy said.

"Oh yes! Cream puffs!"

"You're evil," she replied, but took the bag.

"And you're too thin. Like, it's time to be drinking Ensure too thin." Nikki smacked herself on the flank. "Someday, when you grow up, you might possibly top out at over a hundred pounds, and then people will start to take you seriously."

Cathy laughed. Yes, *that* was the problem, oh yes indeed, no one took her seriously. Ha!

"Soooooo," Nikki said, sitting down and drinking Cathy's milk, "have you jumped Shirtless Ken yet?"

"I'm pretty sure that's not his real name," she teased.

"Avoid the question a little more! So, I'm guessing no."

"You would be guessing correctly. In addition to his many other odious qualities, which are legion, he drinks."

"Oh."

"A lot."

"Well, drinks like, hey, come in and have a beer? You know, like normal people? Or drinks like, hey, come in and help me finish this keg?"

"I have no idea because, thankfully, I don't know him well enough to make that judgment. He mentioned losing his license the other day. DUIs."

"Ouch. Still, that doesn't mean he'd, you know, suck in the sack."

Cathy rolled her eyes. Neither rain nor sleet nor substance abuse would prevent Nikki from pushing inappropriate partners on a friend. "Thankfully, I have no idea if that's true."

"Well, get on it, Cath. You've gotta strike while the bird is in the bush."

"And you've got to stop mixing your metaphors. I cannot *believe* you're pushing me toward this man, whom you know perfectly well is totally inappropriate for me. For any right-thinking woman."

"First off, real people don't say 'whom.' Stop saying 'whom.' Second, what? Like you've got so many great other options?"

"There is more to life," she said sternly, "than sex."

"There *is?*" Nikki looked shocked, which made Cathy laugh again. "Get out!"

"I'd like to, but this is my kitchen."

"Yeah, brag a little more, creep. I still can't believe you actually own property."

"I can't, either," she confessed.

"I suppose you're already plotting to redo the fence? Dig up the garden? Fix the gate?"

"Yes, yes, and yes."

"And the fact that you don't know a drill bit from a dildo isn't going to stop you?"

"Well, no," she said, and burst out laughing.

"Just checking." Nikki downed a cream puff while prowling around the main floor, eventually pronouncing it, "Absurdly neat. Finished unpacking already, huh? Yech."

"We can't all take eighteen months." Cathy shuddered. She'd helped Nikki move last winter and the woman *still* had boxes stacked all over the guest bedroom. "Seriously, Nikki, how about if I come over and—"

"No no no no no no *no*."

"No?"

"You're *not* coming over and unpacking for me. No way! I can never find a damned thing after you've cleaned. You have to hide everything."

"I did not hide the vacuum cleaner," she replied sharply. "It was in your hall closet—an eminently suitable location, I might add, and—"

"Blah-blah-blah. So, what are we doing today?"

Cathy sighed. Nikki was annoying, blunt, rude, infuriating, and her oldest friend. She would do well to keep in mind that Nikki put up with *her* personality quirks as well. And almost always without complaining. Well, sometimes without complaining. Well . . .

"I didn't know we were doing anything today," she replied. "What did you have in mind?"

"Going over to see how badly Shirtless Ken is hung over," Nikki said promptly. "Then invite him out to lunch. Let's take him to one of those No Shirt, No Shoes, No Service places, just for fun."

Cathy laughed again, unwillingly. The most annoying thing about Nikki—and this was really saying something— was her completely absurd way of looking at life. Because she had not been joking. "How about we don't do that, instead?"

"Oh, fine, you pick, then." Nikki took off her baseball cap—the one with the puzzling yet eternally fascinating logo GOT MAMMARIES?—fiddled with her long, straight blond hair for a moment, then tucked it all up under the cap. It never ceased to amaze Cathy how much hair Nikki managed to hide. Normally it hung down to the statuesque beauty's waist.

Maybe that's why Nikki saw all her friends as beautiful, Cathy mused. Because she herself looked like an escapee from a *Sports Illustrated* swimsuit issue. Ridiculous, but there it was.

"As long as it's something fun," Nikki was ordering. "Which means *no* libraries, *no* bookstores, and *no* bed-and-breakfast tours."

"No tractor pulls, either."

"Like I'd go to one in this heat," Nikki retorted, which was, Cathy felt, entirely beside the point.

Chapter 7

"Ooooh," Nikki said when they pulled into Cathy's driveway four hours later. "Company."

"God *dammit*," Cathy said, and pulled the emergency brake with a yank. Nikki's car, a standard transmission, promptly stalled. Annoying habit of Nikki's Number 672: the woman insisted on being driven everywhere. "I told him. I *told* him."

"Uh-oh. I'm sensing a personal space violation."

"How the *hell* did he get in?"

"Whoa with the potty mouth! A 'dammit' and a 'hell' on the same day? Cripes. Poor slob doesn't know who he's messing with."

"You're right about that," Cathy snarled.

"Now Cath. I'm sure"—Nikki said, scrambling out of the

car and hurrying after her—"he's just trying to help. You should be, um, flattered."

"Flattered?"

"Okay, intensely annoyed. Aw, come on, give him a break . . . he's so cute!"

"People have been making allowances based on his appearance his entire life, I've no doubt." Cathy pushed the front door open and practically leapt into the foyer. "I have had enough."

Her worst fears were realized: Shirtless Ken had lugged a stepladder, tool box, and various implements that required plug-ins into her living room. He was currently up on the ladder, poking a screwdriver at her 123-year-old chandelier.

Which he had offered to fix the day she moved in.

Which she had politely refused.

And now he had snuck, had waited until she was gone and *snuck into her home*, on the pretense of "helping" her, and that was . . . that was just really . . . that was . . .

"Ken!" she bawled, and later decided that's why she felt such guilt and why she made the series of disastrous decisions. Because if she hadn't yelled, the rest of it might never have happened.

Startled—which was stupid, hadn't he heard them drive up?—Ken flinched. The screwdriver went in a little too far. Shirtless Ken was suddenly galvanized as electric current slammed through him.

Cathy had just enough time to start toward him and think, *don't touch him, knock him off the ladder with something wooden—*

a broom?, when he toppled off the ladder and hit the living room carpet so hard a cloud of dust rose in the air.

"Holy shit!" Nikki had time to gasp, before Cathy seized her arm in a claw-like grip. "Ow!"

Then Cathy hissed, "9-1-1!"

While Nikki grabbed for her cell phone, Cathy crossed the room, seized Ken by his shirtless shoulder, and hauled him over on his back. His eyes were open, staring at nothing. His chest didn't rise and fall. There was blood on his face, blood had foamed from his nose, but it wasn't moving, wasn't leaking. It was just there.

Cathy did not pray—she believed in God, but felt He had a strict "every man, woman, and child for themselves" policy—but she had time to think, Please God, not another ghost in this place. Then she started mouth-to-mouth and CPR.

"Well, he was clinically dead for a good minute," the doctor told her an hour later. "Lucky for him you were there, Miss Wyth."

"I don't think he's gonna see it exactly that way," Nikki cracked. Cathy shot her a look and the taller woman immediately stuffed the rest of the Hershey's bar in her mouth. "Gmmf nnnf unnf."

Cathy took a deep breath and faced the resident. "How long will he be here, doctor?"

"Well, we'll keep him overnight for observation," she said. She was a short woman who was probably twenty-five but looked forty-five. Sleep-deprived didn't begin to cover it. She blinked at Cathy through glasses that made her look like a tired owl. "But you can take him home in the morning."

"*I* can?"

"Yes, he's listed you on all his forms."

"But I'm just his neighbor!"

"Well, now you're his home health aide, as well." The doctor must have noticed the way her eyes were bulging out of her head, because she added, "You're surprised."

"That's one word for it," Nikki said with her mouth full.

"But Ken seemed very sure that you—"

"Have my friend here right over the proverbial barrel." Nikki started to laugh. "And to think," she added with typical irrepressibility, "I almost stayed home to watch the *Seinfeld* marathon!"

Chapter 8

"So how's your stud-in-a-bed?" Nikki asked. She was standing with odd respectfulness outside Cathy's screen door.

"He's sleeping," she replied shortly. "What are you doing out there? Come in."

"Well, you *did* kill the last guest who took you by surprise," Nikki said, opening the screen door and stepping inside. "I'm the cautious type."

"My ass," Cathy said rudely.

"Oooh, more profanity! A new and, may I say, dark side of you. So, how's Shirtless?"

"Asleep. Don't you have a job?"

"And miss all this? No chance, Killer."

"Do *not* start calling me that."

"Okay, okay, don't get mad, Psycho."

"Oh, God . . . Nikki . . ."

Her friend—ha!—took pity on her and set a bag bulging with bakery goods on the table. "Brought breakfast! And seriously, Cath, I thought you might need a hand the first day or so. So, I told work that my grandma died—"

"Again? Nikki, they're bound to do the math one of these days—"

"Minor details. So here I am, with three days off at your disposal. Paid!"

"God help me. I mean, thank you." Cathy pulled the bag toward her and opened it. Ah. Cream puffs, éclairs, smiley-face sugar cookies. Bakeries were divine. The one down the street, Rosie's, in particular. "I guess this works out nicely. I had some vacation time I needed to burn or I'd lose it, so I've got the rest of the week off, too."

"To play nursemaid?" Nikki asked, reaching for an éclair and decimating it in two bites.

"I . . . guess so."

"Mm innfff afff oo, y'mmmmf."

"I know, but what could I do? Abandon him at the hospital? He almost *died*, Nik. He did die, actually, for a few minutes."

"Zzz mmm nnnt."

"I know, I know, but I think the punishment was quite a bit worse than the crime, don't you? And I'm *not* being taken advantage of," she added sharply as Nikki opened her mouth to drool custard and make another point. "He might have put my name on the forms, but it was still my choice to have the ambulance drop him off here. In fact, don't you think that's sad? That out of all the people in the world, he listed a neighbor? Not even an old neighbor. A new one. I just—I just hope everybody's okay with it."

Jack hadn't made a sound since the accident. No helpful plates of cookies, no materializing car keys, no knocks. Nothing. Zip. It was funny how something initially scary had gotten comforting. His silence was making her distinctly nervous.

"Well, shoot, Cathy, I didn't think my opinion mattered so much," Nikki joked. "Hey, the only one who has to be okay with this is you. Me, I think you're nuts. But I've thought that since the seventh grade."

"Continuity," she mused. "How comforting."

"Amen," Nikki said, and selected a cream puff. "So, is he asleep or what?"

"I don't know," she confessed. "He was sleeping when the ambulance dropped him off. I've . . . I haven't gotten around to checking on him yet. The doctor said he needed lots of rest."

"Is he burned?"

"Not too badly. The shock was pretty quick. He's got some second-degree burns on the tips of his fingers and his feet and that's about it."

"He's likely to be a sucky patient. You know how men are. Okay, *you* don't, but take my word for it, they're total babies when they need to be taken care of."

"That's a cliché."

"For a reason, honeybun. Trust me, this guy's gonna be a pill."

"I suppose," she sighed.

"Well." Nikki popped the top off her cream puff, like

taking the cap off a mushroom, and carefully licked out the whipped cream. "Go check. Get it over with."

Cathy drummed her fingers on the table and glanced at the stairs. "I suppose. The alternative is watching you eat."

"Hey, I got a bag full of cream puffs, honey. I could do this all morning."

Cathy got up to check on her new patient.

Chapter 9

She rapped softly on the guest room door, heard nothing, and carefully eased the door open. Shirtless Ken was sitting up in bed, smiling at her. The fact that it was a genuine smile and not a leer was startling in itself, but there was something different about him. Not just the smile. Some fundamental change in his appearance, something she couldn't quite put her finger—

"Nice shirt," Nikki observed from behind her.

Ah-ha!

"Good morning, Nikki." Ken's smile widened, showcasing laugh lines around his gorgeous dark eyes. "Good morning, Cathy. I'm sorry to be so much trouble." His voice was deep and soft, and gone was Shirtless—er, Ken's—usual sneery whine.

"No problem," Nikki said, staring.

"I'm just so sorry you got hurt," Cathy added. Ken was wearing a scrub top, doubtless loaned to him from someone at the hospital. His dark hair was mussed, and stubble bloomed along his jawline. "I feel . . . I feel . . . I feel . . ."

"Terrible," Nikki supplied helpfully.

"That is simply ridiculous, ladies," he said. "I can assure you the accident was entirely my fault. Why, I'm fortunate you're allowing me to stay here at all!"

Nikki stared at her watch. "How long has he been asleep?" she muttered. "What year is this?"

A fine question. Cathy was having a terrible time not staring. Not drooling, to be perfectly blunt. If Shirtless Ken had been ridiculously good-looking, Polite Ken was mesmerizing. Those dark eyes . . . almost knowing in their intensity, their—

"Really," he was saying, "I can't thank you enough."

"D'you want me to run over to your place, pick up some clothes or something?" Nikki offered.

"I couldn't put you to more trouble, Nikki."

Cathy cleared her throat. "Can I—would you—are you hungry?"

"Starving," he said softly, looking her straight in the eyes.

"One, two, three, swoon," Nikki said under her breath.

"I'll . . . I'll bring you some soup."

"Perhaps I should get it," Ken suggested. "I feel I'm imposing on you enough as it is."

"Don't be a dumbass," Nikki said. "You're supposed to

rest. We'll be back in a second. Don't so much as twitch out of that bed."

For a second, before she shut the door, Cathy thought she saw Ken blush. But that was ridiculous. The man threw epithets around like he was being paid for them.

"Oh my God," Nikki was rhapsodizing on the back stairs. She clutched her chest and wheezed like an asthmatic on the first day of spring. "Talk about turning over a new leaf! You should kill people more often!"

"Maybe he feels bad. What kind of soup do you think he'd like?"

"Maybe you have a helpless hunk in your bed and should stop babbling about soup. Those eyes! That hair! Ooh, the sexy unshaven look! God, he looks like an escapee from Studs and the Women Who Make Soup For Them."

"Tomato?"

"Cathy, I swear to God . . ." Nikki slumped into the closest kitchen chair. "Did you see the way he looked at you? All earnest and yummy?"

"Earnest and yummy?" she repeated, laughing in spite of herself. "Actually, I'm relieved. I thought he was going to be . . . ugly. Very ugly." In fact, she had been dreading the confrontation. "It makes logical sense; he was unpleasant *before* I accidentally killed him."

"Ken couldn't be ugly if you drew a mustache on him in black marker. Hell, red marker. I'm gonna go up and see if he needs a sponge bath."

"Nikki . . ."

"I was only going to do his testicles," she whined.

"Nikki, make yourself useful." Cathy tossed her friend a sponge. "And it's not what you're thinking. The dish soap is under the sink."

"Sure, while you tempt him with soup, you whore!"

"That's the plan," she replied smugly.

Chapter 10

"Really, Cathy, I can feed myself," Ken teased. He gently took the spoon from her, and she nearly tipped the bowl over at the shock of his warm fingers on hers. "I feel terrible to be putting you to so much trouble. The least I can do is dribble soup down my own chin."

"It's . . . it's no trouble."

"Well, I know you must have a job to worry about."

"I took some time off."

"Now I feel even guiltier," he said softly, but he smiled at her and she nearly drooped into a puddle beside the bed.

"They'll . . . they'll just have to get along without me at the office for a couple of days."

"This is very good, by the way."

"It's just . . . it's just from a can."

"Homemade chicken soup is overrated," he said, and

laughed. Laughed! A deep, booming laugh that made her smile. She'd never heard him really laugh before. Sneer and chuckle nastily, yes. But a true laugh? "I used to hate my mother's chicken soup. She'd take a perfectly good chicken and wreck it with vegetables and overcooked noodles."

Cathy pounced. "Should I call her? Do you have *anybody* you'd like me to call?"

Ken's smile faltered. "No. No, there's no one. I'm the last of my family line."

"Oh. I am, too. Except for my father and his wife. I'm . . . I'm sorry."

"It's not your fault, Cathy. You've got to stop apologizing for events you can't control."

"Okay." She took the plunge. "But, um, but the fact that you're here flat on your, um, back for the week is very much my fault, and I—"

"Now, Cathy, we've been over this. I was stupid, and I paid the price. I'm grateful for the use of your guest room, and promise I won't be a burden on you much longer."

"You're not a burden," she said truthfully. She couldn't believe she was thinking it, much less saying it, but she added, "It's nice to have company. I'm still not used to living in such a big house by myself."

"You weren't really by yourself, though." He scraped the last of the noodles from the bottom of the bowl, then handed it to her.

"What?"

"Old houses have stories," he clarified. "Histories. It's hard to feel alone when you're in the middle of history."

"Oh. Hmm. Uh-huh. Ken, are you on any medication that I, as your hostess, should be made aware of?"

"Gosh," he said, handsome brow knitting in thought. "Not that I know of. Maybe some, what do you call them, antibiotics? You can check the bag the hospital sent me home with, if you like."

"Because you don't seem yourself. At all." Thank goodness! Still. Very odd. She'd been bracing herself for Sullen Shirtless Lawsuit Ken. This smiling, pleasant stranger in Ken's body was a complete shock. Argh. She shouldn't say shock.

"I know I seem different, Cathy," he was saying. "But there's a reason for it."

"There is?"

"Yes, of course. You've given me a second chance at life. I don't plan to waste it this time."

"Nikki helped."

There was something warm on her leg. She assumed he was experiencing a moment of incontinence, then realized he had rested his hand on her knee. "You're lucky to have a friend like Nikki," he was saying, "but she's not really my kind of girl."

"Oh yes? You mean the tall, gorgeous, fearless type? A real turn-off, huh?"

"I like them smart and petite, with cheekbones you could cut yourself on."

Totally weirded out, she moved her now-sweaty knee away from New and Improved Ken. "Oh. Well. That's, um, nice. Would you like more soup?"

"I think I'll rest now, if you don't mind."

"Okay." She stood. "Just, um, yell or something if you need anything."

"Of course. Thank you again for the fine lunch, Cathy. But it's Cathleen, isn't it?"

"What?"

"That's what it is, for real."

"Nobody . . . I mean, everyone calls me Cathy."

"Yes, but Cathleen suits you better."

"Okay. Have a nice nap."

Completely mystified, she walked out, feeling his gaze on her until she closed the door.

Chapter 11

"Okay," Nikki was saying as Cathy not-so-ceremoniously shoved her toward the door, "*I* have an annoying neighbor, too, and while he isn't quite as yummilicious as Ken, he's definitely got potential, so if you could just come over and kill him—" She teetered on the steps, and Cathy gave her one more gentle shove. Arms pinwheeling, Nikki went down. "Aigh! All right, all right. At least think it over, willya?"

"Good night, Nikki." She shut the screen door, then locked it for good measure. Friends, she added to herself. The ultimate mixed blessing.

And speaking of friends, she'd been missing one lately.

"Jack?" she whispered in the kitchen. "Are you there? It's okay if you've been hiding because of all the ruckus lately, but it should settle down soon."

Nothing.

"And me without my car keys," she joked, which was a lie, as she knew right where they were. Still, Jack had been unable to resist finding them before.

Nothing. Dead silence.

She gave up and climbed the stairs to bed.

Cathy woke hours later, scared out of her wits and not understanding why.

Then she realized why: her bed was shaking. Not trembling, not twitching, *shaking*. It was sliding forward, then would slam back against the wall hard enough to nearly throw her to the floor. Then the performance would repeat. And repeat.

"Jack!" she screamed, clutching wildly at the bedsheets. "Jack! Stop it! Jaaaaaaaaaaaaaack!"

The door to her room was thrown open and there was Ken, walking calmly toward the madness. "I apologize for not knocking," he said as he bent and scooped her up.

"You shouldn't . . . you shouldn't be up. You have to rest; the doctor said you have to rest. Don't let go of me," she begged.

"Never. Besides, I can't sleep in this noise," he pointed out, kicking her bedroom door shut behind them. She could still hear the thumping of her bed, but it was growing fainter . . . either because Jack was getting tired, or because Ken was taking her so rapidly, efficiently away from the noise.

"There, now," he said, tucking her into the left side of his bed.

"He's never . . . he's never been like that before," she said, almost gulped. Why were silly things like bouncing beds so terrifying when it was dark out? She'd probably be laughing about it in the morning. "I know you'll think it sounds silly, but he's—"

"Houses have history, remember?" he asked, climbing into bed beside her.

"Um . . . Ken . . ."

"Don't worry," he said, kissing the tips of her fingers, then releasing her and rolling over on his back. "I know you're not that kind of girl."

I'm not?

"Thanks for coming to get me," she said softly in the dark.

"I'll always come to get you," he replied, and she supposed that should sound creepy, like something out of the Stalker's Handbook, but instead it was so darned comforting she fell right back to sleep.

Chapter 12

Ken was gone when she woke up, thank God, because Nikki was standing over her, leering. Needless to say, a startling way to begin the day.

"Don't start," she said shortly, throwing back the quilts and standing. Atypically hot spring or not, her toes instantly froze to the floorboards. Socks, her kingdom for wool socks! "I mean it, Nik."

"Oh, I don't think so, Slutty McGee. Normally your cool exterior would be off-putting, but not today! Here I am, coming over early to help you with your own personal Ken doll, and I find you in his bed!"

"It wasn't like that, Nikki. He—"

"That's the worst part! I know it wasn't like that; I can't *believe* it. You can't even be loose right. Dope. Otherwise you two would be having a little morning fun, uh-huh, uh-huh . . ." Nikki wiggled her butt for emphasis—like any was needed—

in concert with her eyebrows. "And instead, you're in here snoring like a beagle and he's in the kitchen doing the dishes."

"He's doing the *what?*" Then, "I don't snore."

Nikki held up a hand. "Scout's honor, baby. How many slumber parties have we been to? You snore like a beast. None of us can figure out how such a tiny person makes such a big scary noise."

"Cathleen! Nikki!"

"That's him," she said, looking toward the open doorway. She hurried across the hall to her room and grabbed a pair of sweatpants and a T-shirt. "That's Ken, calling us."

"Well, duh," Nikki said, and slurped her coffee from the mug she was holding. "Thanks for the exposition. Oh, and is that what you're wearing to seduce wayward boytoys these days? The holes over the left knee are an especially attractive touch. Was it barf green when you bought it, or did it just get that way over repeated washings?"

"Breakfast!"

"I hate you," Nikki sighed, following Cathy out the door.

"Well, I hate you, too," she pointed out reasonably. "Besides, I told you, it's not like that."

"Uh-huh. Still hating you—whoa!" Nikki ducked, and just in time, because the portrait she'd passed by in the hall suddenly hurled itself to the floor, missing her by inches. "You need bigger nails, girlfriend," she said, picking up the picture and leaning it carefully against the wall. "Ugh, what is it with the poor slobs in these old-fashioned portraits? Why do they all look embalmed?"

"They didn't have instant flash back then," Cathy explained. She stood on tiptoes to see over Nikki's shoulder. "They would have to hold a pose for twenty minutes. That's why you never see anyone smiling in old pictures."

"More important, why is it still hanging here in your hallway?"

"The last owner left quite a few of her things behind. I told her I'd work on getting them packed away, nicely and neatly. It's part of the reason I got such a good deal."

"Those are the Carrolls," Ken said from behind them, making both women jump. He pointed his spatula at the stiff-looking family. "They built this house. That was the father, Jerome, and that was his wife, Janice. They had two children: Victoria and Jefferson."

"That's enthralling," Nikki said. "Really, and I mean that. I'll take my eggs over easy."

He smiled at her which, stupidly, made Cathy feel jealous as hell. "Yes, Nikki, and good morning. I also have some nice fried ham, and chocolate milk."

"Baby, that's a date!" she cried, sashaying past him into the kitchen.

"How did you know about the family who used to live here?"

"My neighbor," he said easily. "Victoria is the one who sold the house to you."

"I-I never met her. I just met with her lawyer." She distinctly remembered Ken referring to Victoria as "that fucking old bitch." Cripes. He really *did* turn over a new leaf. Maybe Nikki had a point. Maybe she should electrocute men more often.

You need more sleep, she told herself. When Nikki starts to make sense, it's time to go to the doctor for some nice pills.

He came closer—luckily it was a *gigantic* hallway—and brushed one of her dark curls out of her eyes. "Did you sleep well? After the . . . unpleasantness?"

"Like the dead. I mean, like a log. I mean, thanks for coming. Coming to get me, I mean. I would have been scared to be here by myself."

"There's nothing to be scared of as long as I'm here." Then he colored, which was odd to see on such a large man. "Not that I'm planning to overstay my welcome. I just . . . just wanted to set your mind at ease, is what I meant to say."

"Well, I'm sorry if I scared you. Screaming like that. Like an idiot."

"As a matter of fact, you *did* scare me. I was relieved to find you weren't being murdered."

"No, just haunted."

"Yes, about that. I think—"

"I don't want to talk about that right now," she said nervously.

"Well, I'm ready to talk when you are. Like I said, I just want to set your mind at ease."

"And *I*," Nikki said, poking her head around the corner, "want you to set my stomach at ease. Come on, you two can make goo-goo eyes at each other later. Cook, boy, cook!"

"Sorry," Cathy muttered, but was gratified to see Ken hide a smile.

Chapter 13

"Girlfriend, you are eggless."

Caught dreamily contemplating Ken's shoulders, Cathy blinked. "What?"

"Eggless. Egg free. You're out. You got no more. And you're low on milk. *And* you're ugly."

"She certainly is not," Ken said, offended.

"Tell me," Nikki sighed. "Try going to a club with her sometime. I looooooove being 'the funny one.'"

"Shut up," Cathy said, blushing. "Well, I suppose—"

"I'll go to the store," Ken quickly offered. "That is, if Nikki will let me use her car. Mine's . . . um . . ."

"I thought you lost your license," Cathy said. "Too many DUIs."

"Oh. Well, no. But I don't have a car of my own. Anymore."

"Shoot, you can borrow mine. I'll come with you!"

"She doesn't like to drive," Cathy explained.

"It's not that I don't like it," Nikki said, pushing back her chair, "it's that it's the most mind-numbing chore on the planet. I'd rather garden. Or shave a goat. Seriously."

"Let me get my wallet," Cathy said.

"No, I should—"

"Ken, let her pay, she can afford it. Stingy cow has the first nickel she ever made."

"I do not! But Nikki's right," Cathy said, practically forcing the dreadful phrase past her teeth. "I'm supposed to be taking care of you."

"So you don't sue her for this lovely house!"

"And the least I can do is pay for groceries," she added, glaring at her friend.

Ken laughed. "I'm not going to sue you."

"Sure, say that now," Nikki replied. "Cath, I think you've got more potatoes in the cellar." A hank of blond hair escaped from her cap, and Nikki absently tucked it back up. "You're just low on dairy stuff."

"Would you mind running down to the basement and getting them, Ken? I—"

"I need to change my shirt," he said abruptly. "Nikki can do it."

Nikki's eyebrows arched, and Cathy knew how she felt. Since the accident, Ken had been so polite and soft-spoken, it was odd to hear him actually refuse to do a favor.

Nikki shrugged. "Your shirt is fine. Let's go, handsome. Shotgun."

"What?"

"Never mind. Back in a few, Cathy. Make yourself useful while we're gone and, I dunno, do the dishes or something."

"Oh, hush up," she muttered.

TWO HOURS LATER

She was wiping down the counters, vainly hoping Jack would make his presence known, when she heard the unmistakable sound of a car stalling, starting, stalling, and jerking its way up the driveway. She stepped out onto her front porch in time to see Nikki roll out from her door like a paratrooper in a World War II movie.

"What the hell?" Cathy began.

"The ground, I kiss the sweet sweet ground of life!" Nikki yowled, and then proceeded to do just that, smacking the turf with her lips. Cathy heard the car's engine stall, and then Ken got out and stood awkwardly beside the car, anxiously watching Nikki roll around the yard like she'd been knifed in the dairy section. "My life flashed before my eyes! Six times! And let me tell you, I need to date more!"

"I guess I'm a little out of practice," Ken explained, reddening.

"A little! You're a wheel psychotic with absurdly well-built delts! You're a—"

"Nikki, calm down." Cathy helped her friend off the grass. "For heaven's sake. You're not exactly an expert behind the wheel, either, all the chauffeuring we all have to do for you. Serves you right."

"I nearly *die* and it serves me right? You suck!"

"Are you"—Cathy put up a palm to cover her twitching lips—"all right?"

"Just a little humiliated," Ken confessed.

"You should be a little *concussed*, the way you cut off that school bus!"

"Nikki, you're getting hysterical."

"Damn right I am!"

"I am sorry," Ken said again. "I won't drive you again until I'm better at it."

"Now with the threats," Cathy teased. "Who do you think will get stuck with the duty?"

Ken slipped an arm around her waist and, surprised, she let him. His tentative hug was nothing like his earlier, beery gropings. "Next time you should come with us," he said. "Keep me out of trouble."

"Oh, barf," Nikki said, and stomped into the house.

"You forgot the groceries!" Cathy called after her, and got the one-fingered salute in return.

Chapter 14

"So are you going to jump his bones or what?"

"Aaiigh!" Cathy nearly fell out of the easy chair. "Nikki! I thought you went home!"

"Yeah, well, I forgot my magazines. So I'm back. So? Are you?"

"Keep your voice down."

"So, no."

"None of your business." Cathy lowered her voice to a whisper. "Besides, he's recovering from dying."

"That's always your excuse for not getting laid." Nikki said this in a perfectly normal tone of voice.

Cathy burst out laughing. "Be quiet! He'll hear you."

"Oh, yeah? Where is he? Scrubbing your grout? Cleaning out your fridge?"

"He went to bed. He's tired and his burns were bothering him."

"What burns?"

"They're faint," Cathy said defensively, "but painful."

"Yeah, yeah, whatever. So why don't you go up there with some, I dunno, salve or whatever. Minister to him, like."

"You've been downloading too much porn again."

"I live alone; what *else* am I going to do? And what are you waiting for, dumbass? Seduce!"

"He's a little shy."

Nikki snorted.

"Now, I mean," she amended. "In fact, he's practically like another person."

"Yeah, so, he saw the light at the end of the tunnel and jumped off the track before it could run him over, or whatever. Good for him. Seduce!"

"I'm not you, Nikki." She did not say this defensively; she was what she was. "I can't just go up there and strip and stand on his bed like Venus on the half shell."

"When was the last time I did *that?*" Nikki had finally gathered up the last of her magazines and was impatiently jingling her keys. "Look, Cath, it's not just that he's gorgeous. Although he could definitely give Tom Cruise a run for his money. Plus, unlike certain ex-spouses of Nicole Kidman, Ken's not short."

"We're getting off the subject."

"We never left it, baby! It's just that you don't seem . . . I mean, you're kind of lonesome. You've got your house and your temp jobs and your weekly duty phone call and once in a while I manage to drag you out of here and go to a club and that's all." Nikki faltered; she preferred to hide her emotions behind wisecracks. "And I-I just think you could use something else, is all. And he seems like he really likes you."

"Seems like he really likes me? You should write get-well cards."

"Blow me, how's that for a card?"

"Nikki, don't you think you're being just a bit inconsistent? After all, you were pushing him at me when he was a tiresome blowhard."

"Cathy, that's totally the definition of consistent. Besides, now he's *not*. So what's the problem?"

"That it's gauche to take advantage of someone relying on my hospitality?"

"Picky, picky. Besides . . . whoops!" Nikki dodged just as another family portrait fell off the wall and slammed to the floor hard enough to crack the glass in the frame. "Cripes, how many of these things do you have around here?"

"Lots," she admitted. "Mind the glass. And I'll think about what you said, Nikki."

"Liar," she said, not unkindly, and started to leave, carefully sidestepping the broken glass. "I'd help you clean up, but you know, that's just not me."

"I know she's a pain," Cathy said after she heard Nikki's car vroom off. "But stop throwing pictures at her, Jack. I mean it, now. You've been sulking for ages and now you're acting in a distinctively unpleasant manner. Don't make me call an exorcist!" How, she thought, does one call an exorcist, anyway? The Yellow Pages? Word-of-mouth referral? "Stop it *this* minute."

Or what, she thought, but nothing else happened, so she was spared having to think about it. Instead, she finished *Chicken Soup for the Haunted Soul*, and went to bed.

Chapter 15

Cathy lay awake for a long time. It was late. Past 2:00 A.M. Waking had been a little like dreaming, or swimming: inch by inch through consciousness until she was completely awake, with no idea how she had gotten there, or why.

Then she heard it. Low, guttural moaning. So low and quiet it took her a minute to realize she was hearing anything.

Ken. It was coming from Ken's room.

She got out of bed at once, her feet freezing on the wooden floor, and hurried out her bedroom door and down the hall. A picture swung ominously as she passed it, but didn't fall.

Ken's door was open and she stepped inside without hesitation.

"Ken? What's wrong?"

No answer. He had torn the sheets free of the bed and they were balled up around his middle, and his fists were working restlessly through the cotton. Moonlight fell across the bed and she could see the sweat sheening his body.

She stepped to his bed and shook his shoulder, which was as rigid as stone.

"Don't go in the basement," he said very clearly, and his eyes popped open. Cathy nearly screamed, and in shock her hand clamped down on his shoulder, probably hurting him. His eyes. It had been like looking into the eyes of a dead man.

"K-Ken? Are you all right? I heard . . . heard . . ."

"Cathy, thank God," he muttered, and pulling on her hand, pulled her to him until she was beside him in the bed.

"Are you all right?" she whispered as he stroked her face.

"I am now," he replied. "Stay with me."

"*You're* sort of staying with *me*," she teased to cover her nervousness. She heard an odd sound, then placed it: pictures swinging against the wall in the hallway, but not falling. Jack must not be up for a full-blown temper tantrum tonight. "But sure. I'll stay."

He leaned in and kissed her so softly, it was almost tentative. She was a little surprised—she hadn't expected Ken to be tentative between the sheets, ever—but pleased. She had never been one for a big choking tongue being rammed down her throat. Little butterfly kisses were more her style.

She sat up and pulled her nightgown over her head. "Don't start," she told him before he could. "I'm well aware I look like an extra in *Little House on the Prairie* in this thing."

"I like it," he said seriously. Then he laughed. "It beats what I wore to bed today."

"Yes," she murmured, tracing her fingers across his shoulders, circling his nipples. "We've simply got to go over to your place tomorrow and get you more clothes."

"Tomorrow," he said.

"Yes. Tomorrow."

"Butterfly kisses," she said dreamily, half an hour later.

"Pardon?" She was cuddled against him, spoon-style, and he was kissing the back of her neck and shoulder.

And that wasn't all he had kissed. Even now, she could still feel his mouth on her—well, his mouth *was* on her—and shivered. He had been all hands and mouth and tongue, all hungry skill and silent desire. When he had finally entered her, he had done so because she had been begging him to. When he was inside her, she had locked her ankles behind his back and never, never wanted him to go.

They had rocked together for an eternity, one that was over much too soon. Not that she wasn't ready to be done— she had stopped counting climaxes after six—but beyond the physical pleasure, the *connection* they had shared was so intense, she didn't want it to end.

It had never been like that. She had never *dreamed* it could be like that.

Now they were sweating lightly in the cool dark, and she could feel beard burn where he had kissed and licked and sucked her nipples. She welcomed the mild discomfort. It proved what had happened was real.

"You're so beautiful," he said. "I've always thought so." He reached out and tugged at one of her curls, watching as it bounced back. "But not very many people know how clever and funny you are. It's like a wonderful secret."

"I don't know that it's a *wonderful* secret," she began.

"But you're so quick to denigrate yourself. Why is that?"

"I-I don't know. Nikki's the pretty one, the funny one. I'm just . . . me, Cathy."

"Nikki has her charms," he agreed, "but she's not you."

"Definitely not," she agreed. "Never mind. How come you weren't so nice before I killed you? We could have gotten together a lot sooner."

He didn't say anything, and she cursed herself. "I'm sorry," she said quickly. "That was in poor taste."

"No, that's fine," he replied, obviously meaning the opposite. "I-I have no excuse for how I acted earlier. I was . . . I didn't . . . things were different then."

"Well, all right." She could see how tense he had become; the forearm she was lying against had become hard as iron. "The important thing is, you're here now."

"Yes," he said. "I'm here now."

She leaned forward and kissed him, savoring his mouth, his sweet, firm mouth. He caressed her curls for a moment, then kissed the tip of her ear and cuddled her more firmly into his side.

As they both drifted back to sleep, Cathy had a passing thought that shocked her and left her rigid and wakeful for the next hour.

She had been, in her defense, a little distracted at the time. But while they had been rocking together, while his delicious cock had filled her up, had stroked sweetly, while her hands groped and held and groped some more, while his face had nuzzled into the crook of her neck, she had started calling his name.

And he had covered her mouth. Gently, but firmly. Covered her mouth so she couldn't say anything.

In an instant, she had it. And was furious it had taken her so long to catch on.

My God, she thought. I'm sharing a bed with a dead man.

When she knew he was deeply asleep, she slipped out of his bed.

Chapter 16

"I just want to see Miss Carroll for a couple of minutes," Cathy explained. "I called earlier? Cathy Wyth?"

"Oh, yes . . . Wyth. Well, of course Miss Carroll is always happy to have visitors. It's down the hall on your left, Room 326."

Cathy thanked the nurse and hurried down the nursing home hallway. She had been afraid that tracking down the original owner of her house would be tricky, especially since Victoria Carroll did all her business through her lawyer. But it only took a few phone calls.

Miss Carroll was a surprise. For one thing, though she was sitting in a wheelchair by the window, she was perfectly erect, and her hands, slim and pretty, were busy with a pile of knitting.

For another, she was beautiful. Not "gee, I can see she was

pretty when she was younger" beautiful. Beautiful-right-now beautiful. Her long hair was unbound and flowed over her shoulders and back, and was pure white. Her face, while heavily bracketed with laugh lines, was porcelain pure, with a wide forehead and a narrow, foxy chin. Her eyes were the green-brown of a pond in the deep woods.

"Hello," she said, looking up from her knitting. "How are you liking the house?"

"Oh, you . . . you know who I am?" Cathy was cursing herself for making assumptions. Just because the older woman chose to do all her business through a lawyer didn't mean she was lacking, either mentally or physically. "I mean, I—"

"The desk announced you. And your name was on all the paperwork I received this week. Would you like a pop? Some coffee?"

"No, I-I just wanted to . . . I was just interested in your family."

"My family." Miss Carroll commenced knitting, her bright purple needles flashing in the morning light. "My family is all dead, Miss Wyth. All except for me."

"Yes, I . . . yes." Cathy sat on the edge of the bed, suddenly feeling foolish. Where was she supposed to go with this? Hi, thanks for selling me your house, I think it's haunted? And what was Victoria Carroll supposed to *do* about that, exactly?

"I'm ready to go," she continued. "I've been ready for a long time. I never had any children, never even got married. I miss my brother, and I miss my parents. I'm ready to go home."

"Your brother?"

"Mmm. Jefferson. Oh, that was a terrible day."

"A terrible day?" Then, "Jefferson?"

"We were horsing around, you know, like kids do—although we didn't think we were kids *then*, certainly not—and my brother was home from Harvard. He was so happy to be home! He said nobody on the coast could cook like our mother, and we started chasing each other. It was so silly and childish. Then he tripped on the basement stairs." Miss Carroll dropped a stitch, then stopped knitting altogether. "There wasn't a mark on him, isn't that strange? Nobody could get over it. How handsome he was at his funeral, like he was sleeping. But his neck was broken and that was that. One minute we were laughing and tearing around, and the next we were planning a funeral."

Don't go in the basement.

"So Jefferson . . . your brother . . ."

"Oh, he's the ghost living in your house." Victoria Carroll was looking right at Cathy; no hiding behind knitting this time. "I was so upset. I blamed myself for his death for years and years. Couldn't leave the house, never got married. Never had a life outside of my family's, and once my parents passed on, there was . . . nothing. And I guess my brother stayed around. Looked after me. He always hoped I would move on. And I did, just a couple of weeks ago. But I think . . . I think the habit of staying in the house, it was too strong." She paused. "We always called him Jack, you know."

It was a good thing, Cathy decided, that she was sitting down. Because she felt as if she were falling. "No," she said faintly. "That's not how it works. You're supposed to have no idea what I'm talking about, and I'm supposed to help you sort of work around to it, and then it'll be this dramatic revelation, not a . . . not a matter-of-fact story where you just blurt out, oh, by the way, the ghost is my brother Jack. Didn't you know?"

"Sorry, darling, but I don't have that kind of time."

"I guess I'm the one who's sorry. I sort of assumed you . . . you wouldn't know what was going on. But you do know."

"I honestly thought he would either leave when I sold the house," Miss Carroll said, "or come with me. I wasn't tricking you. I have to admit, I kind of miss him. How is he?"

"He's taken over the body of my obnoxious next-door neighbor. And now my neighbor is the ghost." Cathy sighed. "I should have kept renting."

"Oh." She brightened. "So he's alive again?"

"Well . . . yeah."

Miss Carroll clapped. "Wonderful!"

"No. My neighbor . . . he's stuck in some sort of limbo, he's—"

"You're not talking about Ken, are you?" Miss Carroll's mouth thinned with distaste. "I wouldn't worry about *him*, dear. Anything that happened to him, he had it coming."

"Yes, but he's *in my house*," Cathy said, exasperated. "Living with a ghost might be business as usual for you, Miss Carroll, but it's a pain in my ass!"

"Well, yes, if the ghost is Ken. Jacky was a *wonderful* ghost. So helpful."

Cathy flopped back onto the bed. "My head hurts."

"You're just Jack's type, too," Miss Carroll commented,

picking up her knitting. "All that dark curly hair, those big eyes . . ."

"Don't start on my curly hair and big eyes, please. What should I do?"

"Marry my brother," she said promptly.

"About. The. Ghost."

"Oh, I'm old so I know about exorcisms? Call a priest, dear. Or don't. Ken struck me as the type who withers without attention. He'll probably go away on his own."

"You know, there's the small matter of your brother taking over a body that didn't belong to him."

"Bullshit," Miss Carroll said. "Jacky was cheated out of his own lifetime. Dead at twenty-one; you call that reasonable? What was Ken doing with the body, anyway? Riddling it with STDs? Filling it with alcohol and getting DUI's? Using it to date-rape unsuspecting women? Why shouldn't my brother have a chance?"

Because it was wrong. Because the body didn't belong to him. Because it was creepy. Because she didn't mean to kill Ken. Because nothing was that simple. "I . . . I don't know."

"Exactly." Miss Carroll held up her knitting, then reached into the bag at her feet and withdrew a new ball of yarn. The yarn exactly matched her knitting needles. "Give my love to Jacky when you see him."

Chapter 17

Cathy slammed into her house and stomped into the kitchen. "You've got a lot of explaining to do, buster!"

"Yeah!" Nikki added, wiping up the last of the egg yolk on her plate with her toast. "What are we doing?"

"Nikki, go away. This is between me and Jack. And don't park in my spot anymore; I almost rear-ended you this morning."

"Uh-huh. His name is Ken, dear."

"Hush up. Go to the bakery. Go to the bathroom. Something."

"You figured it out." Ken-Jack looked absurdly relieved. And adorable, with the dish towel slung over one shoulder. He smelled like Dawn detergent. "I thought you might. I've been trying and trying to think of how to tell you—"

"My ass!"

"Ooooh," Nikki said.

"You've only had a million chances to bring it up and you blew it every time. How about after we made love last night, buster? Huh? How about then?"

"Jesus, I can't leave this place for one night without all hell breaking loose," Nikki commented.

Jack put his hands on her shoulders, dark eyes serious. "Cathy, you're right."

"I *know* I'm right. I'm not an idiot. Nikki?"

"That's right," she said. "She's not an idiot."

"I meant go away."

"I should have told you," Jack was saying. "But to be honest, I couldn't think how. I was afraid I'd scare you. There just isn't a nice way to say 'when Ken died I took over his body' without sounding like a bad man. And I would never want you to think I was a bad man. I love you, Cathy. I'd do anything for you."

"Oh. Well . . ." She chewed on her lower lip. "You're kind of taking the wind out of my sails, here . . ."

"Let me get this straight," Nikki began. "Your house was haunted by this guy, who, when you killed Ken off in a fit of rage—"

"I did *not*—"

"—took over Shirtless Ken's body. Well, who's knocking down all the pictures?"

"Ken," Cathy and Jack said in unison.

"Man, no wonder he's pissed. Not only did you steal his body and put the moves on his girl, he's now relegated to the spirit world and stuck in this termite trap? Bogus!"

"You're taking this awfully well," Cathy said suspiciously.

"I'm the one who keeps getting almost eye-gouged with flying glass," Nikki reminded her. "And Ken *was* an asshole. This whole passive-aggressive crap would be just like him. It makes sense, sort of."

"I want you to know," Jack said, his hands still warm on her shoulders, which was unbelievably distracting, "that I didn't take over Ken's body. I was sort of . . . sort of pulled into it. You'll never know and I don't have the words . . . I was so happy when I woke up in the hospital. I couldn't believe I'd been given a second chance after all these years. A second chance—"

"Ugh, don't say it," Nikki warned.

"—with you."

"Okay, I'm officially barfed out now."

"Shut *up*, Nikki. Really, Jack?"

"Why else do you think I wanted to come back here? Not just because I grew up here. I wanted to be close to you. When my sister moved away, I thought it would be my time to just . . . leave. But then I saw you . . . you looked so . . . so lost and so determined. And you were so pretty . . ."

"And don't forget about her cute split ends."

"Nikki!"

Jack laughed. "I even liked your friend."

"Did you like me, or did you *like* me like me?"

"*Nikki.*"

"And I-I couldn't leave. When I heard you talking on the phone with your family, I thought, this woman is alive, and she's as lonely as I am. And I just . . . couldn't leave you."

"Thanks," Nikki commented. "Thanks a lot. What am I, chopped liver?"

"Nikki, get it through your head: this is not about you." She looked back up at Jack. "I went to see your sister today, Jack. She told me everything. About what happened to you in the basement. About why you never left her."

"I'd like to go see her, too. If I could just get you to drive me—"

"*That's* why you're a shittier driver than me," Nikki said. "You're about a hundred years out of practice!"

"Not quite a hundred," Jack said dryly. "It's—"

"Basement!"

Jack flinched. "Don't do that."

"Okay. Basement!"

"I'd kill her, except I get the feeling she'd never leave," Cathy said, glaring at her friend.

"What are we going to do about Ken?" Nikki asked. "We can't just let him hang around knocking pictures off the walls."

"What is this 'we' stuff?" Cathy asked. "And frankly, I have no idea."

"It's very difficult to manifest," Jack said quietly. "If I affected something in the physical world, it would often take days to build my strength back up. And I had things to hang on for. My sister, for example. Ken . . . Ken has nothing but his anger."

"Well, he was a pretty angry guy . . ."

Jack shook his head. "It's not enough. It's really not." He

squeezed Cathy's fingers. "Love is. Love can last for years. Anger . . . anger wears off."

"Barf again. So he'll just . . . just fade away?"

"Something like that."

Relieved, Cathy said, "As long as he can't hurt anyone on the way out."

"You could take a vacation," Nikki suggested. "You've already got the time off from work. Go to an island or Disney World or something. Maybe . . . get to know each other. I bet when you come back, Ken will be long gone."

Jack smiled. "What a wonderful idea."

"I agree," Cathy said. "Plus, if we're not here, we won't have pop-in guests every third hour."

"What, I'm not going with you guys?"

"Forget it, Nik."

"Nikki, you're very nice," Jack began tactfully, "but—"

"No you're not," Cathy said. Impulsively she squeezed Jack so hard his eyes bulged. "Besides, this is me-and-Jack time. No pals allowed."

"So that's it? You're gonna take off with a guy who's been haunting your house for a zillion years? A guy you barely know? That's not like you, Cath."

"I know," she said, and smiled at Jack.

Paradise Bossed

For Daniel and Lisa,
who introduced us to the real paradise
that is Little Cayman.

Also, thanks to the Cannon Falls Bombers,
and all those pep rallies back in high school,
which have made the Cannon fight song stick
into my brain like a fishhook.

AUTHOR'S NOTE

The events of this story take place about a year and a half after the events in "The Fixer-Upper" (*Men at Work*, Berkley Sensation anthology, December 2004). Also, snorkeling is usually a harmless activity.

Cannon, Cannon, loyal are we.
Red and black we'll shoot you to victory.
So fight fight fight our motto will be.
Rah-rah-rah and sis-boom-bah!
Fight fight fight fight!
Go for the red and black!

—CANNON FALLS HIGH SCHOOL FIGHT SONG

You'd bitch if they hung you with a new rope.

—ALEXANDER DAVIDSON III

"I see dead people."

"In your dreams . . . while you're awake? Dead people like in graves? In coffins?"

"Walking around like regular people. They don't see each other. They only see what they want to see. They don't know they're dead."

—FROM *THE SIXTH SENSE*

Prologue

ST. PAUL, MINNESOTA
FEBRUARY 21, 1975

Jack watched with interest as his sister's nosy-body neighbor dragged a GP (General Psychic) into his house.

It was actually his sister's house; it had passed to her on their parents' deaths. But they both knew whose house it really was. Jack had lived there for many years. His sister was getting on, but he felt just the same.

"You can't mean to *live* like this," Nosy-body was saying. "Who lives like this?"

"Well." His sister looked around helplessly, but Jack decided not to come to her assistance, this once. She really did need to learn how to stand up for herself. It was his fault she couldn't, and now it was too late. Forty years too late. But if an old dog like him could learn, maybe she could, too. "Well, we get along fine, Jack and me."

"No, no. You must get him out. You can't have a—a dead thing running amok in your own house. It's—outrageous! Your chakra and your aura are completely screwed up." Nosybody rattled the purple beads around her neck as if to make a point. She was wearing a black T-shirt that had a pair of giant red lips on the front. She was an infant at twenty-seven.

"Well, it would have been Jack's house if he hadn't broken his neck in the basement," his sister said reasonably, and Jack almost groaned. "Really, I think of it as his house."

The medium, who hadn't said a word to that point, was looking around at the carefully kept Victorian with an almost bored look on his face. He was holding hands with a small, curly-haired blond boy, a boy with the bluest eyes and dirtiest green coat Jack had ever seen. The child looked like an angel down on his luck.

"You'll never get the damned thing out," the angel said.

"Think so, Tommy?" The medium, who had the same curly hair (less vivid than the boy's), dirty clothes, and blue eyes, seemed unsurprised at the child's tone and language.

"Dad, you can't do it. Nobody could do it." The child paused, his eyes narrowing with thought. "Maybe Mr. Graham in London. Nobody here."

"Sorry, then, ladies," the medium said.

"But you haven't even taken your coats—"

"If Tommy—"

"Tom," the child corrected, bored.

"If my son says it's a no-go, it's a no-go. He's much stronger than me, you see." The medium offered a small smile, which didn't match his eyes.

"Besides, he's not hurting anybody," the child added, apparently in response to the stunned look on the faces of the two ladies. "He helps you, doesn't he, Miss Carroll?"

"Well, yes, I don't know how I'd get along without my Jacky. . . ."

"Yeah, well, that's the problem," the child said. "S'long as you both feel so strongly about helping each other out, he'll never leave. And nobody will ever get him out."

"Er . . . oh."

"Good-bye," the child said, almost politely.

"Good-bye, dear. Thank you—thank you both—for coming."

"Bye, Jack."

Jack knocked once in response, making Nosy-body jump. The child didn't even turn, and the father was halfway out the door already.

That poor boy! He was, what? Four? Five? And how much of the human condition had he already seen? Murder, sex, greed, thievery, vanity—it made Jack shiver to think about it.

"Not one of my finer moments," his sister said when they had left.

He knocked.

"I know, I know, I should have told Sharon I wasn't interested. Because I wasn't, you know. She just has a way of—taking over, I guess. All that chakra talk makes a lady tired." She paused, waiting, and then added, "And I'd never get rid of you, darling."

Sulking, Jack didn't respond.

"But I must admit I was curious."

Jack restrained himself from snorting.

"And I also have to admit I wanted to meet a famous medium." While she chattered, she set the pot on for tea and rummaged through the cupboards. She was a tea snob, and would no sooner use a Lipton bag than go outside without a girdle.

"Thomas Fillman is supposed to be the most powerful psychic in the Midwest. But I see it's Thomas Jr. who's the real talent. That poor baby! Better at five than his father ever was, and now he's being dragged all over town to dig through old houses, looking for ghosts. . . . I could cry right now."

Well, don't, Jack thought. *It's none of our business.*

Still, he couldn't help wondering, as the years passed, how the child was doing, and if he was happy.

Chapter 1

LITTLE CAYMAN, 2006

Nikki floated through the azure waters beyond Little Cayman like a—well, like an angel, thank you very much! Her long blond hair was fanning out behind her as she twirled and whirled through the water, dancing like a water sprite, wriggling through schools of fish like . . . like . . .

Like someone who's got to get a grip, she thought, and snorted, and then had to swim to the surface.

She spit out the mouthpiece, along with a mouthful of seawater. "Angel!" she crowed, and only the gulls heard her. They spun overhead, laughing at her. Natch! Angel. Shit.

She dipped her head back in the water, skimming the long strands away from her face (ah, they were like strands of kelpy, smelly seaweed, that was romantic, right?), then adjusted her mask and bit into the big rubber nipple.

Then she dove back down to examine the glory that was Little Cayman Island. She should have gone back and re-slathered sunscreen, but dammit, she was having too much fun.

And soon enough, she'd be out here constantly; Pirate's Point Resort wasn't that big—maybe ten guests, total, and most of them on the boat all day. Cathy and Jack, who didn't dive, would be necking all over the place. Nikki felt like enough of a third wheel at home; she had no intention of feeling like that on her vacation.

It wasn't their fault, and they weren't doing anything wrong. Cathy was newly in love, ditto Jack, and after eighty zillion years, Jack was starved for sex, touching, hugging, kissing, even handshakes. A trip to the store to get milk could quickly end up an X-rated straight-to-video incident.

She was nuts to have accepted their invitation—it was their anniversary, for God's sake.

That said, she'd also have been nuts to turn down a free trip to the Cayman Islands . . . although why Cathy had a jones on about coming to a place famous for scuba diving, when neither of them dived, was a mystery. It was like deciding to go to Antarctica when you didn't like penguins, or the cold.

She swam down, wiggling her flippers to get as close as possible to the sea floor. Schools and schools of fish swam by, ignoring her—to them she was just another skinny tourist in a Target bikini. But Christ! It was like being on the Discovery Channel. Fish and coral—live coral, no less—and birds above and turtles below. Unreal. Here she'd been going to Disney World every year, with no idea what she was missing.

She saw something out of the corner of her eye and turned to get a better look, then jerked back, startled. Stingray. Nice-sized, too—a six-foot wingspan. It wouldn't hurt her; rays were huge but gentle, and this one was startled, and as it flinched away from her, the barbed tail whacked her, quite by accident, across the side of her face.

But that was okay, because they were harmless, you just had to watch out for the—for the thing—the thing on the end of their—

Luckily, her face didn't hurt. And the blood in the water—it probably wasn't hers. And even if it did attract sharks, there was nothing in these waters that could hurt her. Not even rays—they only stung you if you stepped on them by accident. That's what her instructor told her, and he knew his shit. Besides, it hadn't even hurt.

No, nothing hurt; everything was numb. She'd figured on swimming up for another breath of air, but she didn't need one now.

She brought a hand up to touch her face and missed. Were her lips gone? Or was she too numb to find them? She swam to get to the surface, and bumped into the ocean floor.

This is not good, she told herself, but really, it was impossible to get worked up over it. It was so beautiful here, so peaceful. She was almost a part of it, lying on the floor in the rich silt, a part of the fish and even the saucy ray who had smacked her by accident and gone on its way.

She pulled off her mask and snorkel. Ah! That was better.

Now she could breathe. It was a lot harder, breathing water than air, but she was up to the challenge.

It was too bad, though. She herself didn't mind so much, but her pal Cathy would completely lose it when she heard the news.

Chapter 2

"What do you mean, 'missing and presumed'?" Cathy shrieked. "What does that mean? Why aren't we looking for her? Why weren't you looking earlier?"

"Is she dead?" Jack asked. "I guess you'd better tell us if she's dead."

"Of course she's not dead, she's just snorkeling. Right?"

"For eighteen hours?" her husband asked gently.

Cathy clawed through her hair, the curly dark hair Nikki so admired. And still did admire! Not past tense: present tense. Nikki was very much in the pesent tense, nothing was wrong, it was all a stupid misunderstanding, that was all, just a—

". . . came alone, and we're pretty casual here. . . . You can keep the snorkeling gear in your room and go out whenever you want. We have no idea when she left, but she wasn't at supper last night, or breakfast this morning, so we alerted the coast guard as well as—"

"Nobody's seen her since last night? Well, we—we—" She cast around. "We have to find her, then. That's all. We just have to. She's a good swimmer but she's not used to the ocean—we live in Minnesota—and she'll be waiting for us to get her . . ." Cathy burst into tears, and was instantly pissed at herself for doing it. This accomplished nothing. It slowed everything down.

Her husband, cool as a flounder in most situations, patted her but fixed his gaze on the guide, waiting patiently for an answer to his question.

"Yes," the guide said with great reluctance. "I think she's dead."

"Of course she is, she's been dead since last night, only she was alone and no one noticed. She was *alone*," Cathy said, and did something she had never done before, and hoped never to do again: she fainted.

She woke up in their room, their little cabana on the ocean. Jack looked calm and unconcerned, but then, he always did. He *looked* like a twentysomething handyman who had to struggle with *Body Art Monthly*, when in fact he was a hundred-year-old intellectual.

"They're still looking," he said, patting her wrist. She saw he'd taken off her shoes and placed her neatly in the middle of the bed. "They'll find her."

"That's what I'm afraid of," she said, and rolled over to bury her face in the pillow. "I'll never forgive myself, never!"

"Honey, I didn't catch that."

She rolled back over. "I said I'll never forgive myself. She came down here *alone* and we were all supposed to be together, only she came down *alone*, and we should have noticed when she didn't come back from snorkeling, we *should* have! Who dies going *snorkeling*, for God's sake?"

"Well," Jack began cautiously, then stopped. It was just as well; what could he have said? He had died falling down the basement stairs. Talk about senseless.

"What if they never find her?" she asked. "What if she gets . . . you know. Eaten."

Jack just shook his head, and she suppressed a flare of temper. Most men would be all "There, there." Jack knew too much, had seen too much. He wouldn't comfort her if he thought it was a lie.

"Well, we're not going anywhere until we find her. Hear that?"

"I hear that," he replied.

"Thank God I quit my job last month," she muttered, throwing a forearm over her eyes.

"I have money," he reminded her.

A bundle. His sister, a lovely woman still living in a St. Paul nursing home, had figured out their secret, and insisted on giving half her inheritance to Jack. Or, rather, the body

Jack now lived in. It had amounted to several million dollars, and had certainly taken the pressure off. No more temp jobs for her, and plenty of money for new carpeting.

The thought of her happiness, of the *money* making her *happy*, when now her best friend was most likely shark supper, made her burst into fresh tears.

Chapter 3

Oh this is so BOGUS.

And not a little bogus, either. Big, gooey, lame bogus. Unendurably bogus.

I hated the movie Ghost. *Demi Moore dripping tears over everything that moved, stupid Patrick Swayze getting his damn self shot, stupid Whoopi Goldberg—well, she wasn't so bad . . .*

Nikki knocked on the cabin door, forgetting, again, that she was incorporeal. The ghost thing was tough to get used to. Worse than passing bio in college!

Her fist passed through the wood of the door and she hesitated. She'd been through three other cabins, looking for Jack and Cathy. This could be lucky number four. That was good, right? Right. Only, she prayed they weren't doing it.

She stuck her head through the door. Success! There they were, Cathy sobbing (nuts) on the bed as if, uh, she'd lost her best friend (okay, she had), and Jack sitting beside the bed, his chin resting on one fist, watching her with a glum look. He was shirtless, in khaki shorts, deeply tanned, and even in the middle of her rather large problem, she noticed for the hundredth time how yummy her best friend's husband was.

Who was tan in March? They lived in Minnesota, for goodness' sake.

"Sorry to ogle," she said cheerfully, "but it's your own fault for letting him walk around without a shirt."

Nothing.

"Guys! I'm okay! Well, relatively speaking."

"I'll never forgive myself," Cathy said, her voice thick with tears.

"You did nothing wrong, love." Jack's voice was a soothing rumble.

"I just can't stand the thought of her floating around out there, all alone—Nikki hates being by herself."

"Uh, guys?"

"Cathy, you've got to stop. You've been crying for hours. You'll make yourself ill."

"Guys?" She walked over to them—she might be able to pass through walls, but an old habit like walking on the floor was hard to break—and waved her hands in front of them. "Guys? I'm here. I'm okay. Relativ—never mind. Don't cry, honey, you know how your nose swells up."

"I can't help it," Cathy cried. "This was supposed to be a fun vacation for the three of us, and now what? The coast guard is looking for my best friend's body."

"They are? Oh, great. I guess." She grimaced at the thought

of gorgeous tropical fish nibbling on her toes. Had she sunk? Was she floating? The salt water was going to be murder on her hair. . . .

"Because of you," Cathy accused. "You just had to finish that damned painting."

"Don't go blaming him," Nikki said sharply. "It was a silly accident."

Jack's mouth tightened for a moment, then he replied, most gently, "Love, Nikki wouldn't want you carrying on like this."

"Yes I would! I mean, you guys can mourn for a day. That's all right."

"I can't help it," Cathy said again.

"You must. It's been a week. You have to try to calm down. You must think of the baby."

"The *baby*?" Nikki almost yelled.

"I'm sorry for what I said," Cathy said. "It was my fault, too. I wanted to stay for the doctor's appointment."

"Baby?" Nikki shouted again. "Oh, nice! You let him knock you up, and you were gonna tell me when? Jerks!"

Then it hit her: a week? But she'd only died a couple of hours ago! Sure, it had taken her a while to get back to the island and find their cabin, but—

"I guess you're right," Cathy sighed, sitting up. Jack got up at once and went to the bathroom. Nikki heard the sound of running water, and then he came back out holding a full glass. "Thanks."

"Drink it all," he told her. "You don't want to become dehydrated in this heat."

"Jerks! I'm in the room, you know. What, you're all done mourning now?" Although, the thought of Cathy crying non-stop for a week (a week?) was sort of dismaying. Especially if she was *el preggo*. "Can you really not see me?"

She stuck her arm through Jack's head. He didn't notice. Didn't even get a cold chill, like in the movies. And the guy had been a ghost himself for, like, eighty years.

She thought of *The Sixth Sense*, the most horrifying movie in the history of cinema. She had been mesmerized. That poor kid. Poor Bruce Willis.

But, what was worse than seeing dead people?

Not being seen at all.

"Jerks," she said again. It was lame, but it was all she could think of.

"Let's go back to the lodge, see if they found—if they found anything."

"You mean," Nikki said, "if they've stumbled across my rotting corpse."

Jack got up again. "You stay here and try to relax." He rested his hand on her annoyingly flat stomach, and Nikki thought, *The true, awful irony of death: I still have cellulite.* "I'll go check."

"Hurry back," Cathy practically begged.

"I will. Rest."

He walked through (yeesh!) Nikki, making her windmill her arms in surprise, opened the door, and was gone.

She rushed to the bed. "Cathy! Cath, it's me." She waved frantically as her friend sighed and gulped and sniveled. "Come on, we're—we were—best friends. There's a bond! There was a bond. Argh. Fucking past tense. You've got to see me."

Cathy groped for a tissue and noisily blew her nose.

"See me!" Nikki yelled. "Dammit! People are scared shitless of ghosts! You're supposed to see my bad dead self and freak out!"

Cathy sighed and stared at the ceiling, tears leaking from her big blue eyes and puddling in her ears.

"Okay, remember this? I was too tall for cheerleading and you were too lame, but we learned the cheers anyway."

She threw her arms up in a V for victory.

Cannon, Cannon, loyal are we.
Red and black we'll shoot you to victory.
So fight fight fight our motto will be.
Rah-rah-rah and sis-boom-bah!
Fight fight fight fight!
Go for the red and black!

She leapt in the air, limbs akimbo. "Yaaaaaaayyyyy!"

Cathy cried harder. Not that Nikki could blame her.

"Dammit," she said, and plopped into the chair recently vacated by Jack. She had so much momentum she slipped through it, through the floor, and a good four feet into the ground, which really gave her something to swear about.

She had prowled every inch of Little Cayman (or maybe *haunted* was the word) and except for the resort guests and the iguanas, there was nothing but sand and nauseatingly gorgeous beaches.

Nothing had changed. Cathy had been crying on and off, Jack had been stoic, the cook had produced magnificent meals, and the coast guard boats kept chugging up and down the beaches, sometimes very close to the dry sand (she was amazed the boats didn't beach themselves, like whales), sometimes little dots on the horizon.

Morbidly, Nikki wondered how much longer they'd search. And where the hell was her body, anyway? Probably in the gut of some damn great white.

She had tried talking, yelling, screeching, cheering, walking through them—nothing. Nobody else on the island could see her, either.

Was this it? No bright light? No afterlife? Just stuck watching her best friend's misery? Even Patrick Swayze got the bright light, after a while. This—this was unbearable. She had never dreamed being dead would be so bad, but watching your friends suffer was hell.

Due to the tragedy of her untimely death, she, Cathy, and Jack were the only guests at Pirate's Point. Everyone else couldn't get back to the small airport fast enough. Nobody wanted to go scuba diving, either—and who could blame them? Everyone was afraid of stumbling across her body.

The iguanas, usually fed fruit by indulgent guests, were getting bad off—certainly Cathy and Jack weren't in the mood to toss grapes at them. The boats stayed tied up; the snorkeling equipment stayed in the shed.

If this went on much longer, the tiny resort would really be hurting.

But Jack and Cathy wouldn't go home. Nikki had no idea how to feel about that. Relieved? Annoyed? If they left, she'd be by herself. But they couldn't keep hanging around Little Cayman until . . . until. That was just . . .

She walked through the south wall of cabin 3 just in time to see a naked Jack climb on top of her (naked) best friend. She had a horrifying glimpse of hairy ass and Cathy's pale flailing limbs before she gagged and lurched back out the wall. Not fast enough, unfortunately, to drown out Cathy's "Jack, Jack! Do it now!" and Jack's rumbly "Ah, my sweet fragrant darling . . ."

"Nice!" she hollered. "I'm dead and you two are boning—again! Or celebrating life. Whatever. Still, take a breather once in a while, willya? It's the middle of the day. Besides, how many times can you get her pregnant in a—a—month?"

How long had it been? Time, she had discovered in death, was a slippery concept. The sun raced across the sky, followed by the moon, and although it only felt like a couple of days, Cathy was already showing.

She decided, trudging back to the lodge, that as fine as Jack was, if she never saw his hairy crack again, she'd be happy forever.

Fragrant darling?

She put the thought out of her mind, quick.

Chapter 5

"I think we should call a medium."

It was chilly in the small hut—the wall unit was going full blast to combat the tropical heat outside—and Cathy pulled a blanket over her legs. "A medium what?"

"A psychic."

"To help us find the body." It wasn't a question. Jack had been on the spirit plane for almost a century; it was natural that he would think of such a thing. "Maybe—talk to Nikki?"

"Maybe. It's something, anyway. Better than waiting for . . . better than waiting."

She stroked his long thigh. "I guess it sounds like a silly complaint, but three months in paradise is too much. And it's no fun without Nikki here."

"Thanks," Jack said dryly.

"I'm sorry, babe. You know what I mean. Everything's, you know, unfinished. I feel like I'm in limbo."

Unseen by both, Nicki stuck her head through the wall and yelled, "*You* feel like you're in limbo?"

"Yes," Jack agreed as if he hadn't been interrupted. Which, in a way, he hadn't.

"Do you know who to call?"

Nikki popped back in. "Oh, we're in a rerun of *Ghost-busters* now? 'Who you gonna call? Nikki-busters!'"

"I mean," Cathy continued, "how do you find a psychic?"

"I know exactly who to call—not the medium, but the medium's intermediate. She can put us in touch. The boy would be"—Jack's dark eyes narrowed in thought—"well into his thirties. Assuming he's still in the business."

"One way to find out," Cathy said, and got up to get dressed.

THREE DAYS LATER

Nikki was gratified to see Jack and Cathy come out of their cabin after the sun had set. She didn't want to risk interrupting another (gag) intimate moment and besides, she had high hopes. It was a full moon (again) and if she knew her spooky movies and Ouija board fiction, it was a great time for spirits to speak to the living.

"Guys!" she said, following them to the lodge. Their footprints sank deep in the sand; she, Nikki observed glumly, left none. "It's still me. Still Nikki. Don't you think it's about time you noticed me? You know, if you can stop having sex for five minutes."

The lodge van, a tasteful serial-killer gray, pulled into the drive, and her friends hurried to meet it.

That was weird. There hadn't been any new guests since— well.

"Let's try a new one," she said, trailing after them like a puppy. "You've gotta remember this one, Cath. We worked on our walkovers for six months to get it right. Remember? We went to Michigan with my folks that time and memorized it? Cath? Remember?"

The van's engine cut off, and the driver and a lone passenger got out. Nikki, focused on her friends, ignored them. She punched a fist through the air and cheered:

Let's give a cheer for dear old Traverse
Come on and boost that score sky high
And let the north woods ring with glory
For the tales of Central High.

She took another breath (force of habit), made a V for victory, clapped, and continued.

And watch out you who stand against us
For we're out to win tonight.
We're gonna add to the glory
Of the—

"God, will you stop making that noise?" the passenger said, clearly irritated. "I've already got a headache from all the plane rides."

"What?" Cathy said.

"What?" Nikki said.

Chapter 6

He was a tall drink, at least six feet five, and thin—too thin, like he forgot to eat regularly. He had a headful of blond, shoulder-length waves—the moonlight bounced off them in a romantic, yet weird way—and the palest, bluest eyes Nikki had ever seen. Pilot eyes. Shooter's eyes. He hadn't had a chance to shave in a couple of days, and the beard coming in was surprisingly dark and coarse.

"Is this a joke? It must be. I fly two thousand miles to listen to a dead cheerleader reliving her glory days."

"Hey!" Nikki snapped. "I was never a cheerleader. Too tall." Then she realized what was happening. "Wait a damn minute. You can hear me?"

"She didn't make cheerleading," Cathy was saying sorrowfully. "She was too tall. But we had fun practicing together.

That's amazing, that you would know that. Did your psychic vibrations tell you that?"

"The only vibrations I get are when I lean up against the washing machine."

"In lieu of regular dating, I guess," Nikki snarked.

"Shut up, what do you know about it?"

"So how did you—Did you study up on her background before you came here?" Cathy was asking.

"Please," the man said, rolling his blue, blue eyes. Then he looked at Jack. "What are *you* doing alive again? That's not your body."

"It is now," Jack said. "It's nice to see you again, Tommy."

"Tom," the man corrected. "For God's sake. I'm too big to be a Tommy."

"This is my wife, Cathy, and—"

"Do you think you can find her?" Cathy interrupted.

"What's to find? She's here."

"Yippee! Finally, someone can hear me!"

"Yeah, lucky me," Tom said sourly.

She jumped up and down in her excitement and he flinched. "Don't. For the love of God, don't do another cheer."

"I wasn't going to." Then she realized what he had actually said. "You can *see* me, too?"

"Yeah. You need to comb your hair."

She nearly reeled from a combination of surprise, relief, and rage. "Hey, at least I'm not sporting three days of stubble, jerk!"

"You mean she's here?" Cathy gasped. Fortunately, the driver had taken Tommy's beat-up bag into cabin 5, and it was just the four of them. "Right here?"

"Yes, and she won't shut up."

"*You* shut up."

"Tell her we're sorry," she begged, "and tell her—"

"She can hear you," Tom said, looking bored. "You just can't hear her."

"Tell her she must move on," Jack said, obviously forgetting the rules.

"Get lost," Tom said to Nikki. "Go away. Scram."

"Oh, suck my fat one," she said crossly. "Who died and made you king?"

Tom grinned, which was startling. It changed his whole face, took years off. Made him look, she had to admit, almost attractive. "Apparently you did."

Chapter 7

Tom had gone from pooped to horny to annoyed to intrigued, in twenty-five seconds.

And normally, nothing would have gotten him out of his hometown (Pontiac, Missouri) just when it started to get perfect out: not the wet, overwhelming heat of summer, not the brown mid-temps of winter. But he couldn't say no to that kind of money, no matter how nice he'd gotten the yard to look.

As usual, it took him a second to figure out who was dead. What was not usual at all was how instantly attracted he was to the ghost. And what wasn't to like? A tall blonde in khaki shorts and a white oxford shirt; pink sandals and toenails the same shade. He knew it was how she pictured herself, the mental image she carried around, as opposed to what she'd actually been wearing when she died. Another surprise: most people saw themselves as unattractive and badly dressed.

And nobody on the other side (that he'd seen, so far) worked on cheers; they were much more concerned with finding forgiveness, or happiness, as opposed to spelling out *S-P-I-R-I-T* with their arms.

Heh.

"Thank you so much for coming," the man who used to be dead was saying. Tom remembered Jack Carroll well: It was seeing him alive in a new body that was surprising. Jack had been dead for decades, devoted to his sister, and stuck in a beat-up Victorian in St. Paul. "As you can see, we have a rather large problem."

"Who are you calling large?" the ghost said crossly.

"Heh," Tom said aloud. It was downright alarming; he couldn't take his eyes off her. He had a dozen questions for Jack and didn't care; the ghost was a thousand times more interesting.

What a damn shame he'd been hired to get rid of her.

"So, what's the problem?" he asked her.

"You mean, besides my untimely demise?" she replied. "I mean, I know how self-absorbed you probably think I am—"

"You and every other ghost I've met."

"Not that you should make snap judgments, but don't you think I'm entitled? Just this once? I mean, I'm dead!"

"And you shouldn't be here," he reminded her, inwardly thinking, *Of all the luck.*

"Tell me!"

"Oh," he said.

"Tell her," Mrs. Carroll interrupted (not that she knew she was interrupting), "that we're so sorry, and we'll do whatever she wants. What does she want?"

Tom waited. The ghost (he groped for the name and found it: Nikki) waited. Jack and Cathy Carroll waited. Finally, Tom said, "Aren't you going to answer her?"

Nikki started. "Oh. Right. I guess I was waiting for you to say 'They want to know what you want,' and then I'd answer, and you'd tell them what I said, and then they'd answer, and . . . you know."

"You don't speak English anymore? You lost your hearing when you lost your head?"

"Okay, okay. Tell 'em I'm fine. You know. Relatively speaking."

"She's fine," he said.

"But boy, this is going to get old, quick."

Normally, yes. He almost literally had to bite his tongue to stop from saying, "Naw, not this time."

"Don't you want to go to your cabin and freshen up, or whatever?"

He had; he'd forgotten his urgent need for a piss and a shower the second he'd spotted her, but now the urges came rushing back. "Yeah," he said. *Oh, you're impressing the hell out of her!* "Yeah." "Naw." *Great!*

On the heels of that thought: *Why do you want to impress a stranger? A dead stranger?*

"Well, I can wait. I mean, it's been a couple of months. What's another hour?" She smiled, flashing perfect American teeth. "I bet you've talked to people who've waited a lot longer."

That was true. But normally he didn't mind in the least making the dead wait. God knew they didn't hesitate to impose on him. But somehow, it seemed particularly awful to keep this woman waiting. Seemed awful to picture her moping around in the sand, hermit crabs crawling through her feet and the wind blowing right through her, and nobody seeing her, nobody at all.

He bit his lip and said, "Thanks. But I can freshen up anytime. You—what do you need?"

She looked surprised. "I dunno. What anybody wants, I guess—to make their budget, to get good gas mileage."

"That doesn't help us."

"Nikki," Cathy was asking, "what happened?"

"An accident," she replied. "I'm getting kind of vague on the details. I guess it doesn't matter, right? Dead is dead."

"An accident," Tom told the Carrolls.

Mrs. Carroll was rubbing her little potbelly and looking anxious. "But is she—but you're okay now? I mean—nothing hurts?"

"Not a thing," Nikki assured her friend. The shorter woman was looking a foot and a half to the left, but Tom didn't have the heart to tell her.

"If this were a movie, I guess we'd start looking for her killer."

"No!" Nikki nearly shouted. "Don't worry about my killer. Stupid thing's probably a hundred miles away by now, anyway. Don't hurt it."

"Shark?" Tom asked, and was immediately sorry when Mrs. Carroll—Cathy—looked stricken.

"Stingray."

"*Stingray?*" he repeated, in spite of trying to spare the Carrolls' feelings. "How'd you manage that?"

For the first time, the dead woman laughed. "Chum, it was just being in the wrong place at the wrong time. And I'm not really prone to that sort of thing."

"Once was the charm."

"Yeah," she said, laughing again. "It was the dumbest thing. You wouldn't believe."

"Try me," he said.

"Maybe later," she replied. "You really need a shower."

Chapter 8

Nikki sat awkwardly on the bed, listening to the shower. Not that she had to stay out in the small bedroom/ living room/ sitting area; she could have popped into Tom's bathroom anytime she wanted. But being dead hadn't made her ruder. Much.

It was oddly comforting, this ritual. Pretending there were important things to do like waiting for guests to clean up. But what else was there to do? She'd assumed he'd wave his hands over her and she'd *poof!* to heaven or whatever. But nothing had happened. He and Cathy and Jack had just stood around, looking at each other. They couldn't even talk, because only Tom could see her.

The shower shut off. She again resisted the urge to take advantage of her ghost powers and stick her head through the door to check out his ass.

It was just about the most difficult thing she'd ever done;

it wasn't like she had a lot of other ways to get her kicks these days. Oh, and it'd be morally wrong.

Speaking of morals, she was trying to keep them in mind as he opened the door and came out, damp and clean and wearing a pair of cutoffs. He grinned when he saw her. "Thanks for waiting."

"What am I supposed to say to that?" she almost snapped, then was sorry, then was annoyed she was sorry. "It's not like I had a choice," she said instead.

The smile fell away. "Right. Sorry."

"Me, too. Being dead makes me grumpy," she joked.

They looked at each other. "I've, uh, this has never happened before."

She blinked, which was interesting. It had to be pure force of habit—what did she need to blink, sweat, pee for? Finally, something good about being dead: no more bathroom worries. "'This'?"

"I don't—I mean, I show up, find out what the d—the spirit needs, the spirit goes away, I go away. I mean, this . . ." He looked around the cabin. "It's almost . . . social."

"Believe me, I'd leave if I could. I think I'm stuck here. Here, the island," she added, "not here, your cabin."

"But you're not," he said, going to his bag and rummaging in it. "You've created this—You're here only because you think you—because you need to be."

Because I think I need to be? She decided to let the dig at her sanity pass. She was sure he didn't know how annoying he came off. *Gee, we've got so much in common.* "I don't *need* to be in the Caymans," she pointed out. "It's just a really nice bonus, being stuck in paradise."

"Obviously, part of you does need to be here." Annoyingly, he paused. "So what do you need?"

"Peace on earth, goodwill toward men?"

"'We're the United States government. We don't do that,'" he quoted.

"Oh!" She nearly jumped through the floor. "Greatest! Movie! Ever!"

He laughed. "You're in love with Robert Redford?"

"No, Dan Aykroyd."

"I've probably seen that movie a hundred times," he commented, gesturing her to move over so he could lie down on the bed. She almost cried; it was so nice to have someone interact with her. Him being a *Sneakers* fan was gravy on the roast. "Two hundred."

"Great concept, great script, great actors," she agreed. "And funny! One of the funniest movies I've seen."

"It was pretty funny."

"'Pretty funny'? Why, what's the funniest movie you've ever seen?"

"*The Sixth Sense.*"

"Oh, boy. You're not serious." She peered more closely at him. "You're serious."

"Totally serious. I get the giggles just thinking about it." And he did; he started to laugh. "Dead people walking around all gory! The shrink didn't know he was one of them! And—"

"Wait, wait. We'll pass over the completely awful scariness of that movie to address this new issue: isn't it basically your life story?"

The laughing cut off like he'd flipped a circuit breaker. "No."

Ah. "I heard Jack saying you were, like, this really powerful psychic. I assume your power didn't just pop into your head when you hit twenty-one, right? You must have been doing this sort of thing when you were a kid, right?"

His jaw had gone tight, but his voice was casual, almost joking. "My power?" he asked. "What am I, in a Marvel comic book?"

Do Not Enter. He might as well have written it on his forehead. She pretended she knew he wasn't joking. "Hon, in case you haven't noticed, our lives—so to speak in my case—are a great big comic book."

He sighed and stared at the ceiling. "Some kind of fiction book, anyway."

"Did they scare you?" she asked quietly. "Do we scare you?"

He knew what she meant and answered readily enough. "No, not ever. Not even when I was a kid. The dead— spirits—don't have any power. They can't hurt us. Me, I mean. If I thought they were being too bossy, I'd just ignore them. Believe me, when you're the only person they can talk to, ignoring them gets results"—he snapped his fingers— "like that."

"Thanks for the tip. Why do you keep correcting yourself and calling us spirits?"

"I, uh, don't want to make you mad."

There was an awkward pause. She squashed the strong

urge to laugh off a serious moment with a bad joke and said, "Tom, that's the nicest thing anyone's said to me since I died."

He smiled, looking down at his lap.

"Please don't do that," she added. "You're the only one who looks at me when we're talking. I never thought—never thought I'd miss simple human interaction so much." She ground her teeth so she wouldn't cry. "It's all so—stupid. If you make fun of me, I'll sic a stingray on you."

He stared at her for a long moment, then shot up off the bed. She assumed the airplane food was disagreeing with him until he said, "Come on," as he strode (well, the cabin was so small he was at the door in a stride and a half) to the door.

"Jinkies, Fred, did you solve the mystery?" She carefully got up—this was no time to go caroming through a wall. "What are we doing? What?"

"Simple human interaction," he replied, and out the door he went.

"Why did we come out here for this?" Nikki asked. "And when did the sun come back up?"

"I need your friends to keep an eye on my body," he muttered, sitting down and pulling his legs into a lotus position. "I might fall over."

"You must be putting me on," Jack commented, watching Tom fold himself into a gangly knot. "It isn't possible."

"What?" Cathy asked. "What is he going to do?"

"Simple human interaction."

"Yeah, whatever fit he's decided to have, it's my fault," Nikki explained to her friends, which was silly because they couldn't hear her. "I overshared and now he's freaked out."

"Mmmmmmmmmmmm," Tom said, shutting his eyes.

"You picked a rotten time to go crazy. Again, not to be all

self-involved, but I'm pretty sure this whole thing is still about me."

"Mmmmmmmmmmm." Tom was still mmm'ing.

"It is impossible," Jack said. "And I do not say that lightly." Still, he didn't sound like he thought it was impossible. He sounded fascinated, like he couldn't wait to see what Tom was going to do next.

Nikki squatted in front of Lotus-Tom just in time to see him stand up. And now there were two Toms: Lotus-Tom and Ghost-Tom.

"How about that?" he beamed, standing over his own cross-legged body. He held his arms out. "That's worth a kiss at least, right?"

She blinked hard, reminded herself she didn't need to do that anymore, and cautiously reached out for him. His fingers closed over hers, warm and strong.

"Oh, boy," she said weakly. "Nice trick." And gave him the kiss he'd earned.

Chapter 10

They were walking hand in hand on the beach, a picture right from an ad agency travel poster, except, of course, neither of them was really there.

Her lips were still tingling from the kiss. He'd seized her so hard she'd nearly bent backward, she'd flung her arms around his neck so hard he'd nearly choked, and they'd mashed their mouths together like teenagers who had the equipment, but not the finesse. It had been the greatest kiss of her life.

What a damn shame.

"So, what's this? I mean, your physical body is back on the beach, but you're here with me?"

"Yup." He seemed abnormally cheerful.

"So you have two powers."

"Yup."

"What's this other one called?"

"Spirit walking."

"I had a pair of those once," she commented. "Easy Spirit walking shoes."

He punched her shoulder lightly. "Hilarious."

She was delighting in everything; his hand in hers, the roar of the surf, the texture of his beard (she'd have beard burn after that kiss, and that was just fine), his scent. Being incorporeal wasn't so bad if you had someone to be incorporeal *with*, and although she knew a large part of her problem had been loneliness, the truth was, she had been lonely before her encounter with Señor Stingray.

She had cried on Cathy's wedding day, but hadn't some of them been tears of jealousy?

"When I was little," he was saying, "I used to go right out to the spirits. I didn't realize until years later that I didn't have to do that, I could see and hear them just fine without having to leave my body. Still, it was fun—a great way to sneak out of the house."

She laughed so hard, she almost fell through the beach. "I'll bet! Leave your body all tucked in under the covers, then . . . *whoosh!* Oh, your poor parents."

He smiled down at her and she was struck again by his extreme height: he had five inches on her at least, and she was not a short woman. And his thinness. Shirtless, his collarbones looked like dull knives.

"You know, you really need a milkshake. And the food here is great. We've got to fatten you up. I mean, doesn't this"—she pinched his incorporeal arm for emphasis—"take it out of you?"

He shrugged.

"Because if it didn't, you'd probably do it all the time, right? And I bet you don't. Do that all the time, I mean." *Oh, God, I said "do it."*

He shrugged again. "It doesn't matter. I wanted to—" He almost choked off the rest of the sentence.

"What?"

"I wanted to touch you," he said, sounding like someone was strangling him. "See if you felt as good as you looked."

She stuck her foot between his ankles and he went sprawling on the beach, and then she pounced on him like a puppy with a new chew toy. "Yeah?" she challenged. "Well, I don't think you can tell by just one lousy kiss."

"Lousy?"

"It was terrible." She rubbed her chin into his chest and ignored his giggles. "Definitely time for a do-over. Remember that? When we were kids, if something didn't go right, you'd get a do-over?"

He stopped laughing. "I was never a kid." Then he cupped the back of her head with one big hand, pulled her down, and kissed her—almost bruised her—and she kissed him back. They were rolling around in the sand like a couple of beached flounders, and she thought, *There's something wrong with him. He's . . . broken.*

When they finished, they were lying inside a tree. "That can't be good for any of us," she said, standing up and automatically starting to brush off the sand—then remembered sand didn't stick to her anymore. She could go to the beach anytime she liked and not have sand get everywhere! Hmm, advantage number two. "Don't you want to get back to your body? Aren't you tired?"

"After *that*? Hell, no." He adjusted the waist on his shorts and grimaced. "Tired is the last thing I feel."

I won't look, I won't look, I—who am I kidding? She stole a peek at his bulging crotch, then said, "Forget it, pal. I'm not that kind of ghost."

"Just checking," he grumbled, and slung an arm around her shoulders, and they trudged back to the lodge.

Chapter 11

"Uh . . . where'd everybody go? And where's your body?"

"Good damned question."

Lotus-Tom was gone. She could see the marks in the sand where he'd been sitting, and there were more marks—drag marks? Like there'd been a scuffle? And then—

"Footprints," she said, and pointed. "Going back to your cabin."

"Mmmm." She could see he was pissed. She didn't blame him. How embarrassing to lose track of your physical body! She could relate. "Lucky for us you used to be a Girl Scout."

"I *did* used to be a Girl Scout, smart guy. Nobody in my troop sold more cookies than I did. *Nobody.* God, what I wouldn't do for a Thin Mint right about now."

He grunted, unmoved by her cookie lust, then marched to his cabin and walked through the door.

Wow! Do I look like that, all cool and vanish-ey? She did the same thing, and, since the cabins were so small (but then, who came to Little Cayman to hang out in their cabin?), nearly walked through the bed as well.

Lotus-Tom had been put on the bed, his legs untangled. And someone—Cathy, probably—had tucked the covers up to his chin.

"For God's sake," Ghost-Tom said.

Jack, sitting beside the bed and rereading *Your Essential Life*, didn't look up. Of course he didn't. But it was nice that they'd posted a guard.

Ghost-Tom was climbing into Lotus-Tom, who immediately sat up on the bed and said, "Don't ever do that again."

Jack dropped the book. "Don't ever do *that* again. I'm an old man; my heart can't take it."

"Spare me." Lotus-Tom—er, just Tom, now, she supposed, threw the covers back and climbed out of the bed. "I know you meant well, but it's really, really disturbing to come back to where you left your body and then have to look for it, all right?"

"Aw, get over yourself, ya big baby," Nikki commented helpfully, grinning when he shot her a glare.

"My wife was worried about you. She wanted to get you indoors, as there was no telling when you'd return to your— when you'd come back. So we brought you back here. Not without difficulty, I might add. You're a lot heavier than you look."

"Ohhh, snap," Nikki said.

"I have big bones," Tom said sulkily.

"My wife is resting, but I'll go wake her if you found anything out."

"Found anything out?"

"About Nikki," Jack said patiently. "About how to help her."

"Uh . . ."

"Go on," Nikki urged. "Tell them you used the time to find out what a great kisser I am."

"It's a long and complicated process," Tom said.

"How can you *lie* like that?" she almost shrieked.

"I'll have to spirit walk a few more times to get to the bottom of this."

"Yeah? Well, you can make out with a hermit crab for your pains, chum."

"So," Tom finished cheerfully, "no need to wake up your wife."

"Oh." Jack bent over and picked up his book. "As you wish. She'll be relieved you're back. Is Nikki okay?"

"She's fine," Tom said.

"I'm *fine*? Buster, the next time I can touch you, I'm giving you *such* a kick in the balls. . . ."

"You missed supper—and lunch—but I can go get you something from the lodge."

"Not hungry," Tom replied. "That's fine, take off."

"Are you sure?" Jack was lingering by the doorway. "I don't think I've seen you eat since you've gotten here."

"Oh, I had some crackers on the plane. Now shoo."

"Good advice," Nikki snapped, and marched through the wall.

"I didn't mean *you*!" she heard him yell after her. Too bad.

Chapter 12

She had avoided the lot of them by lurking—haunting—the other side of the island. And she'd learned a crucial thing: no matter how powerful the psychic was, a ghost could hide from him if she really wanted to. And she really wanted to.

But, after sulking for a couple of days she decided to go back to the lodge side, just to check on Cathy if nothing else. And there was nothing else. Certainly she'd never care if she ever saw Mr. Makeout again.

There were a number of coast guard boats tied off and quite a few people milling about the lodge. Another unmarked van was idling in the driveway, and something in a big bag was being loaded into it. Nikki had a sickening feeling she knew what it was. And why Cathy and Jack weren't there.

She carefully walked into their cabin only to find the three of them sitting in odd postures. It took her a minute to put her finger on what they were doing, and then it hit her: they were waiting.

"It's about damn time!" Tom snapped by way of greeting. He had, more's the pity, put on a shirt today to go with his cutoffs. Then, to her friends: "She's here."

Cathy's eyes were rimmed in red; she looked like she'd been playing with the wrong color eyeliner. "Nikki, they found—they found you today."

"Yeah, I gathered from all the ruckus."

Silence. A dead silence, one might say. Then Cathy added timidly, "So I guess she can go on, now?"

"Go on *what*?" Nikki asked.

"Cathy and Jack think that now that your body's been found, there's no reason for you to keep haunting them."

"I'm not haunting them!" she yelled. "How many times do I have to say it? I'm stuck, but I'm not haunting. I *want* them to get on with their lives, crissake, what's it been, three months?"

"Four and a half," Tom corrected her.

"Right! My point! Tell 'em I said to get lost! Go back to their lives! Bye-bye, Charlie!"

Tom blinked, then turned to Cathy. "She says finding her body made no difference. She wants you to get back to your own lives. She wants you to leave."

"But—but she's still here."

"Yup," he agreed.

"Look, if I could poof on to heaven or the next plane or the next life or whatever, don't you think I would have by now? I think—don't tell them this—I think I'm stuck here because *they're stuck here. I'm not haunting this place*, they are."

"She thinks your refusal to move on is why she's trapped here."

"I told you not to tell them!" she howled.

"My God, that's awful," Cathy gasped. "But—but tell her we can't just leave her here in limbo like this."

"Then she's doomed," Tom said. "Sorry to sound dramatic, but there it is. She can't move on if you can't move on."

Cathy bit her lip and looked down at her lap. Jack patted her arm with one hand, and tapped the nightstand with the fingers of his other hand, an obnoxious habit he had when he was thinking about something difficult.

"Besides, she won't be alone," Tom added. "I'll stay here. You know, help her onto the next plane, all that stuff."

"What?" Nikki was appalled, intrigued, and appalled all over again. "You don't know what you're talking about."

"Oh—you will?" Cathy brightened. "You'll stay with her? That's different. I mean—now that they've found the body—there isn't anything else for us to do. At least she can see you, talk to you."

"Right! Well, half right. Good-bye! And take *him* with you."

"Shall we discuss your fee? Because—"

"No, no." Tom waved that away. "The fee you already paid is more than I make in six months. That's fine."

"Well." Cathy bit her lip again and looked at her husband. "I guess we'd better pack."

Nikki walked back outside before Tom could hear something she might regret. They were doing what she wanted, right? They were

(abandoning)

leaving her, right? It's what she wanted all along, to have a chance to

(be alone)

pick up the pieces, to let them

(live)

get back to their lives.

So how come she felt so shitty?

They packed. Took the van. Flew away. The other van (she assumed it was the coroner's van, if such a tiny island had such a thing) left. The coast guard left. Everybody left.

And now, finally, new guests were coming. She supposed that was a good thing, for the lodge at least. But she sure didn't like seeing strangers in what she thought of as Cathy and Jack's place. Guests who never knew she had existed, and certainly didn't care either way.

And she got what she wanted, right? Cathy and Jack had moved on. Her body had been found, identified, claimed, and, by now, buried next to her parents in the Hastings Cemetery. Everything was as fine as could be, under the circumstances. Right? She'd missed her own funeral, but who'd want to go to that anyway? Right?

Tom stayed. And because he was the only one she could

talk to, she swallowed her anger and started speaking to him again.

"So, did they get back okay?" she asked.

"It speaks!" he cried. He had sat down in one of the chairs and was pulling off his sandals; now he threw them in the corner and leaped to his feet. "Is it Halloween already?"

"Har-de-har-har. I was just wondering if my friends made it back okay."

"They're fine. Do you know how long I've been waiting for you to get over your mad-on? A damned month!"

"Oh, it hasn't been that long."

He muttered something. It sounded like "fucking dead people."

"What?"

"Spirits have no sense of time. At all."

"Oh. Well, this spirit doesn't, anyway."

"And why were you mad, anyway? Was it so awful that I liked spending time with you and wanted to do more of it?"

"I just think you should have told Jack the truth, that's all."

"That I spent half a day making out with you instead of doing my job?"

She giggled; she couldn't help it. He looked so aggrieved. "Maybe that *is* your job, American Gigolo."

"Sure. Right." He went to the bed, sat on it, became Lotus-Tom, and then Ghost-Tom stood up out of him. "So!" he said cheerfully, carefully climbing down (she could relate—if you moved too fast, you went *under* the cabin) and approaching her. "How about another kiss for your favorite psychic medium?"

"Did you say psychic or psychotic? And how about not?"

She fended him off with a hand under his chin, trying not to giggle. "Is that all you've been thinking about? Being a ghost and making out?"

"Well, yeah," he admitted, knocking her hand away and grabbing for her, causing them to fall through the chair, the wall, and into the bathroom. "Pretty much."

"Have I mentioned I really like you shirtless? In fact, you should go shirtless all the time. Pantsless, too."

"Ditto." Their clothes (were the clothes incorporeal, too? must be) went flying (through the bathroom wall!), and she was kissing him with wild kisses, kissing him the way a desert survivor drank water, kissing him and loving being touched, being caressed, being groped. He wanted her at least as badly as she wanted him, so there weren't any flowers or candles or tenderness, just two bodies urgently trying to get into the same place.

She groaned as he entered her, but when he gritted "sorry," she responded by wrapping her legs around his waist and pushing back.

"Sorry, save your sorry and fuck me," she muttered, and his hand slapped the tile beside her head and curled into a white-knuckled fist, and he shivered over her.

"Better not say that again," he groaned, "or we'll be done right now."

"So one of your powers isn't stamina?"

He groaned again and laughed at the same time, and their stomachs slapped against each other as they quickened to some internal beat, a song only they could hear. She wouldn't come, of course, she was the kind of woman who needed at least ten minutes of foreplay, but that was all right, because just being touched, being with him, was enough for—

She came. She came so hard she thought the top of her head would come off. And he was right there with her the whole time, and he never stopped touching her, and she never wanted it to stop, not any of it, not ever.

Chapter 14

"Look at this," she said, picking her shirt up and putting it back on. "Is it a real shirt? Why do I have to put it back on?"

"You don't."

"Funny. But why do we even have clothes? Are they ghost clothes? Why am I always in this shirt and these shorts?"

"Because that's how you saw yourself—casually dressed, comfortable, attractive."

She touched her hair and tried to look modest. "And you said the dead have no sense of time—how come?"

"You're not ruled by clocks like the living. How long have we been stuck in that shitty bathroom, making love?"

"Half an hour?" she guessed, stepping into her shorts.

He looked wounded. "All day. We missed the lunch bell and the supper bell."

"Oh. Well, it was a great day," she assured him. "Don't you want to go eat?"

"I'll stay here with you."

"Both of you?" she asked, a little creeped out. Here was Ghost-Tom, strolling around naked, and here was Lotus-Tom, sitting like someone frozen to the bed.

"I can only touch you in this form," he said quietly.

"Yeah, but Tom, you've got to take care of your—your living body."

He shrugged, indifferent. "Want to go for a walk?"

Yep. Definitely broken. "Uh, sure. But it's no problem to wait until you've eaten. Hell, I probably won't even notice if you leave for half an hour; it'll seem like thirty seconds to—"

There was a rap on the hut door, which Tom ignored. Nikki, being the kind of person who always had to answer the phone or the door, stuck her head through the wall and said, "It's the manager. Don't you want to answer it?"

"No."

"But it might be important."

"Is he holding phone slips?"

She peeked again. "Yes."

"It's just job offers."

"Job offers?"

"Jobbbb offffers, arrrre youuuuuu haaaaaving trrrrouble hearrring meeee?"

"Very funny. You're turning down work to hang out with the dead girl?"

He shrugged; a maddening habit, but eloquent. "Your friends paid me plenty."

"But still. Don't you want to get back to work?"

He looked at her. "No."

She was surprised to discover that a ghost could blush. "Oh."

"So how about that walk?"

She smiled. "Sure. I'd love a walk. I can show you all the places I've been haunting."

He laughed. "Two ghosts, no waiting. Wouldn't the tourists just shit?"

"What if one of them is special, like you?"

"Nobody's like me," he said simply. Not bragging; stating fact.

"Well, that's the truth."

"Say it twice," he said smugly, and held out an arm, and escorted her through the wall.

Chapter 15

"Tom . . ."

"Mmmm?"

They were in the pool, walking around in the deep end holding hands. It was a riot! They both ran and jumped to get momentum, and here they were. Nikki kept holding her breath from force of habit, then remembering and letting it out with a whoosh, which Tom found endlessly amusing.

"This has been a great couple of days—"

"Three weeks," he corrected.

"Right. And it's been awesome. Don't get me wrong. But . . . when are you going to go?"

He frowned at her. "Go?"

"Yeah, you know. Hop a plane, get back to your life. You must have one."

"A plane?"

"A life."

"I like it here," he said, sounding wounded.

"Well, yeah, but Tom—you can't just stay here indefinitely with me."

"Why not?"

"Why *not*? What do you mean, why not? You just can't! It's not like we're a normal couple. I'm dead, for crying out loud."

"So?"

She stopped walking and pulled her hand out of his. A pair of legs appeared in the shallow end and she had a *Jaws*-eye view of the swimmer.

She ignored it and addressed the (rather large) problem at hand. "Let me get this straight. My problem was Jack and Cathy couldn't move on, and now it's that you can't move on? You're not eating, you're not taking work, you're in limbo just like me."

"Just like you."

"No, Tom, that's a *bad* thing. That's why you're so goddamned skinny: You escape your life by hanging out with ghosts. And you lose track of time, just like I do. Have you considered the fact that one of these days you might just starve to death?"

"That would be awful," he said without a shred of conviction.

"Oh, come on! That's not a plan, is it? A seriously fucked-up plan?"

"Would it be so bad if it was?"

"Tom, you have a life! You can't just—just throw it away so we can hold hands and watch the sunset. Come on!"

"Can't we?" he asked quietly.

"You. Have. A. Life. This." She gestured to the legs flailing above them. "Is not. A life. You're alive! You'll be dead soon enough, even if you live to be eighty."

"It's different for everyone," he said, still so quietly she had to strain to hear him.

"What?"

"It's—I think it's whatever you can imagine. If you see harps and angels, that's where you go. If you see hell, that's where you go. If you think you have unfinished business, you stay here. The afterlife—it can be anything. Anything at all. And I don't know if—what if I live to the end of my life and go somewhere else? What if I can't find you again?"

"Are you saying—are you saying that you love me and want to be with me?" Because he hadn't said it. She hadn't, either.

They'd had sex all over the island—once on top of the bar in front of six patrons who couldn't see them.

They'd talked about things, private things, they had never told anyone.

The only thing they hadn't talked about was the future. Because, of course, there wasn't one. Not for them, anyway.

"Because I—" Love you, she started to say, then stopped. Wasn't that making things worse? How could he move on if she told him? And that was the worst of it: four months ago (or six, or eight, or whatever) there had been one ghost trapped on the island.

Now there were two.

"Of course I don't love you, how could I love you?" he cried, and his voice was bitter, so bitter. "You're the same as all the others, why can't I think of you like all the others? You're just one of *them*."

"Them?" But she knew. Sure she knew. Here was Tom, spirit walking with a dead woman because that was better than anything else he had planned for that day, that month, that year. And here was why.

"Just a—just another ghost who distracted my dad. I couldn't get any fucking attention from that guy unless I was working. Do you know what it's like to be eight years old and totally jaded on the human condition, but still want your dad's approval more than anything?"

"No," she said quietly. "I don't."

"Well, it fucking sucks. And you—you! You're just the same, just another dead person who only cares about what she can get so she can move on, just me-me-me, and never mind that maybe my dad and I should have had a life, never mind that there was never enough money in the bank account to satisfy him, there was always one more job, one more person to help, never mind Christmas, never mind my birthday, we gotta drop everything because some idiot didn't look both ways and got creamed crossing the street, and now she's freaking out about not telling her husband about the new checking account."

He paused and gulped in a new breath (not that he needed to in this form, but old habits died hard and if she didn't believe that, just look around her), and she waited for more tirade, but he deflated like a stuck tire. "I guess that's all I have. Your turn."

"Uh, I've got nothing like that."

"Nobody has."

"Now who's being self-involved?" she teased.

"I'm sorry for what I said," he said dully.

"It's all right. I know a lie when I hear one."

He met her gaze with difficulty. "I love you. I'd die for you."

"I love you, too, and I absolutely forbid it. No dying allowed."

They linked hands and walked through the pool wall, through the earth, and up into the sunlight. "You had to work on Christmas?" she finally asked.

"Yes."

"Where was your mom?"

"Dead. She died having me. She was the first ghost I ever saw. She—" He swallowed and she heard the dry click in his throat. "She tried to get me away from my dad, tried to talk me into running away to my aunt's. She wasn't afraid he'd hurt me, just that he'd . . . use me up, you know?"

"Yeah."

"But he was my dad."

She knew. You could never walk away from your parents; they trapped you with sticky webs made of love. You were the fly to their spider. But they only ate you because they loved you.

"Nikki, where's your family? You seemed so concerned about Cathy and Jack—"

"They're my family. I was an only child, and my parents died when I was a freshman in college. Cathy sort of adopted me, you know? We've been friends for a long time."

"What happened to your folks?"

They were walking through the sand now, headed for his cabin. "Well . . ."

"Is it horrible? It's horrible, isn't it?" His fingers tightened over hers. "You can tell me. There isn't a thing I haven't heard, honey, you can trust me on that one."

"No, it's not that horrible, but you'll make a big thing out of it."

"Because it's horrible!"

"It's *not*. Okay, calm down, I'll tell you. Just—don't read into it. It's not a big thing. Okay?"

"*Mmm*. Tell me."

"Well, I was the first person in my family to go to college, right? In fact, I thought that was my name for a while; my mom never introduced me as Nikki or Nicole, it was always 'This is The First Person In Our Family To Go To College.' You could actually *hear* the capital letters.

"So, anyway, we didn't have a pot to piss in, so I got a scholarship and a part-time job, started at the U of M that fall, blah-blah. My parents were so proud; I'd finally made my other name a reality. Then I get a call from Mom's neighbor: big car accident, they're both in the hospital, some dipwad drunk driver ran a red.

"So, I call the hospital—Abbott—and my mom's conscious, but my dad's in surgery and can't talk to me. And my mom's all, 'Don't come, don't come, we're fine, it's finals week there, right?' I mean, she knew my schedule better than I did.

"But I was all, 'Come on, Mom, you guys are hurt, I'll come see you.' And then Mom tells the biggest lie of all: It's nothing, we're fine. We'll call you when we get discharged, come see us after you take your tests.

"And, of course, they died. Dad wasn't in surgery; he was in a coma. Mom died on the operating table. She cheated me out of saying good-bye because she didn't want me to miss my exams. Stupid! Like the school wouldn't have let me take them after the funerals. But Mom didn't know anything about college. Because I was—"

"The First Person In Your Family To Go To College."

"Yeah."

"So. You weren't there for them when they needed you."

"Yes, and I felt tricked and betrayed, and do not be going and making something out of this. It's got nothing to do with what's happening now."

"No, of course not. I'm sure that's not significant in any way."

They were cuddling on the bed now, looking up at the ceiling. Nikki wondered why they bothered—they were incorporeal, they could sleep outside. Heck, they could sleep in a grove of trees and never get bitten by a bug. But old habits.

Lotus-Tom was sitting in a chair across the room. She was used to having two Toms around by now, and scarcely noticed him. "So, back to the business at hand. I love you. And you love me."

"Yes," he said, sounding—could it be? Happy? Well, she'd fix that in a hurry. "I love you and you love me."

"So. You have to go."

"No."

"Yes. Tom, you have to. There's—there's no hope for us. I'm stuck here and you have a life, and if you stay, I'll walk into the ocean and never come back."

"I can't leave you."

"You better. Because I'm not going to have your death on my conscience, Skinny."

"And what kind of a life am I going back to? Being at the beck and call of crackpots?"

"They're not all crackpots," she said quietly. "Some of them need your help. For some of them, you're the *only* one who can help them. You can't turn your back on your life's work for me."

"It's my father's life's work," he said bitterly, "and just watch me."

"Tom. Isn't it bad enough that I'm in limbo? You have to be, too?"

"I won't let you send me away."

"Yes, you will. You know why. I didn't get a chance to say good-bye once, and it's cast a shadow over my life—and death. You have to let me go, just like I have to let you go. That's what all this *is*. There's a lesson to be learned, and I'm by God going to *learn* it this time, you know?"

"No," he said again. He sounded fine, but she could see tears trickling down his cheeks; how they shone in the moonlight! He squeezed her, held her, hugged her hard. "No, no, no."

"Yes."

"Yes."

"Tomorrow."

"No. A week," he begged. "Another month."

"You think this will be easier in a month?" To keep him company, she was crying, too. "It'll never be easier than it is tomorrow—only harder. You have to go. You have to let me go. And I have to let you go. It's the only way we'll be free."

"Freedom is fucking overrated," he said, almost shouted.

"Don't lie to me, Tom. I can spot one a mile away. Now ask me why."

He groaned. "I know why."

"Now ask me how I can let you go."

He picked up her hand, kissed the knuckles. "I know that, too."

They held each other all night and Nikki thought she had never cried so long or so hard, or seen a man cry at all.

And she thought: *your heart can still break when you're dead, oh yes.*

Chapter 16

She waited until he fell asleep, and left. She couldn't watch him leave. If she did, she would weaken, beg him to stay, happily watch as he indifferently starved himself to death, had a heart attack from potassium deficiency, toppled over in bed, and suffocated because he had no one to watch his body. *Whatever, just die and be with me.* Except there were no guarantees that he *would* be with her. And just because her life had been cut short, why should his?

No, she wanted him to live for a hundred years, five hundred, just like she wanted Cathy and Jack and their baby to live for a hundred years. A hundred years at least.

She was going over the same ground again and again (literally; she was on the south side of the island again) and tried to think of something else. Anything else.

She closed her eyes and thought of Tom. His smile, his

rare beautiful smile. His long fingers. His eyes, so wounded and so bright. His skinny legs and bony arms; God, he was scrawny. In her heart's eye, she loved it all, even the way he nibbled on his hangnails when he was distracted.

Tom. You'd better be drinking a milkshake right now. You'd better be—well, if not happy, at least resigned. Happiness will come. It's got to. It—

She opened her eyes.

And managed to just stop herself from screaming in surprise.

The beach was gone. The ocean was gone. She was in someone's living room.

She looked around wildly. Yes, the beach was gone. Yes: couch, coffee table, end tables, chairs . . . this was a living room. She walked over to the window and looked out: traffic streamed by below. And—she *knew* this place. This was Commonwealth Avenue. Boston, Massachusetts.

Boston? But that was where—

She heard keys jingling, locks clacking, and turned around in time to see the door swing open and Tom walk inside, white-faced with fatigue.

Their eyes locked. They spoke in less than romantic unison: "What the hell are *you* doing here?"

"This is my apartment," he said, dropping his bag. On his foot, she noticed, but he didn't notice. "This is where you told me to go."

"But—but—but—but—" She had made him go. She had insisted he set them free. And now she was free. Free to go where she wanted.

What had he said, what had his unique vision of the after-life been?

He slammed the door, curled into Lotus-Tom right there in the living room.

(It's whatever you can imagine.)

Jumped out of Lotus-Tom, raced to her. Kissed her until she thought they'd both topple through the window.

(If you see harps and angels, that's where you go. If you see hell, that's where you go. If you think you have unfinished business, you stay here.)

"I love you, I love you," he was saying, raining kisses on her face, "I love you, but I'm going to choke you for sending me away, I love you."

(The afterlife—it can be anything. Anything at all.)

"I've got some bad news for you," she said, kissing him back.

He held her at arm's length. "What?"

"Well, you have to eat more."

"Done. What's the bad news?"

"Your apartment's haunted. You're my afterlife."

"Oh, that," he said. "Luckily, I happen to be a psychic." And kissed her some more.

Driftwood

This story is, yawningly,
for Cindy Hwang, again, who asked me,
and Ethan Ellenberg, again, who made it happen,
and my kids, who stayed out of the way, mostly.

ACKNOWLEDGMENTS

Stories may pop full-blown into a writer's head, but there's a helluva lot more to making a book than that, or me, the author. There's the editor, who calls you up and asks if you want the project. There's the agent, who wades through the eight-point-font paperwork and looks out for you and points out what's good and what's not so good and why you can't write that story for this guy, but you could write the *other* story for this guy. There are the copyeditors (who think I'm not the sharpest knife in the drawer) and proofers (who think same, and are right) and PR staff (I don't know what they think), the sales guys and gals (ditto), the booksellers (they seem fond of me!), and finally, the readers (it's a toss-up). Pull any one of those people out of the equation and . . . no book. Worse, no royalties!

So thanks, thanks, thanks to the unsung heroes of publishing. Since my name is on the front cover, I get most of the attention and the credit, and the blame if something goes wrong, which is only fair, because it's always my mistake in the first place. But, as above, without the whole gang, there's no book, typos and all.

What would I do without all of you?

AUTHOR'S NOTE

This story takes place after the events in *Derik's Bane* and *Undead and Unpopular*. Also, in the real world, in our world, there are no such things as werewolves, but about vampires, I'm reserving judgment.

Also, the opinions ("I hate kids.") of the characters in this story do not necessarily reflect the opinions of the author, the editor, Berkley Sensation, or Penguin Putnam.

Finally, you are required to let the air out of your tires before driving out on a Cape Cod beach, and the people who don't do that? Deserve whatever happens to their tires.

Who does the wolf love?

—SHAKESPEARE, *CORIOLANUS*, ACT II, SCENE I

He is mad that trusts in the tameness of a wolf, a horse's health, a boy's love, or a whore's oath.

—SHAKESPEARE, *KING LEAR*, ACT III, SCENE VI

A lawful kiss is never worth a stolen one.

—MAUPASSANT

Don't mess with the dead, boy, they have eerie powers.

—HOMER SIMPSON

Burke Wolftauer, the Clam Cop, dusted his hands on his cut-offs and observed the black SUV tearing out onto Chapin Beach at low tide. Crammed with half-naked sweaty semi-inebriated humans, the Lexus roared down the beach, narrowly missing a gamboling golden retriever. It roared to a halt in a spume of sand and mud, and all four doors popped open to let a spill of drunken humanity onto the (previously) calm beach.

All of which meant nothing to him, because the full moon was only half an hour away.

Burke dug up one more clam for supper, popped it open with his fingernails, and slurped it down while watching the monkeys. Okay—not nice. Not politically correct. Boss Man wouldn't approve (though Boss Lady probably wouldn't care). But never did they look closer to their evolutionary cousins than when they'd been drinking. *Homo sapiens blotto.* They were practically scratching their armpits and picking nits out of their fur. A six-pack of Bud and a thermos of Cosmos and suddenly they were all miming sex and drink like Koko the monkey.

All of which meant nothing to him, because the full moon was only half an hour away.

Now look: not a one of them of drinking age, and not a one of them sober. Parked too far up the beach for this time of the day, and of course they hadn't let any air out of their tires. They'd been on the beach thirty seconds and Burke counted an arrestable offense, two fines, and a speeding ticket.

He licked the brine from both halves of the clam shell, savoring the salty taste, "the sea made flesh," as Pat Conroy had once written. Clever fellow, that Conroy. Good sense of humor. Probably fun to hang out with. Probably not too ape-like when he knocked a few back. Guy could probably cook like a son of a bitch, too.

Burke popped the now-empty clam in his mouth and crunched up the shell. Calcium: good for his bones. And at his age (a doddering thirty-eight) he needed all the help he could get.

Then he stood, brushed the sand off his shorts, and sauntered over to the now-abandoned Lexus. He could see the teens running ahead, horsing around and tickling and squealing. And none of them looked back, of course.

He dropped to one knee by the left rear wheel, bristling with disapproval at the sight of the plump tires—tires that would tear up the beach in no time at all. He leaned forward and took a chomp. There was a soft *fffwwaaaaaaahhhh* as the tire instantly deflated and the SUV leaned over on the left side. Burke chewed thoughtfully. *Mmmm . . . Michelins . . .*

He did the same to the other three, unworried about witnesses—this time of year and day, the beach was nearly deserted, and besides, who'd expect him to do what he just did?

He walked back up the beach to retrieve his bucket and rake, using an old razor clamshell to pick the rubber out of his teeth. He belched against the back of his hand and reminded himself he wasn't a kid anymore—he was looking at half a night of indigestion.

Worth it. Yup.

Chapter 2

Serena Crull heard someone come close to her hole and went still and silent as . . . well, the grave.

This was an improvement over what she had said twelve hours earlier, upon tumbling ass over forehead into the eighteen-foot-deep pit: "Son of a biiiiiiiiiiiiiiii . . . ooommpph!"

This had been followed by: "Shit!"

And: "Son of a bitch!"

And: "Ow."

Which had been followed by roughly twelve hours of sulking silence. She had tried climbing out: no good. She'd just pulled more slippery sand down onto herself. She hadn't bothered to try jumping: she wasn't a damned frog. She'd once jumped down, but it was only a story or so and, frankly, it had hurt like hell. Not to mention she hadn't stuck the landing. Jumping up? Maybe in another fifty years.

Then the sun had come up, and she'd *really* been screwed. She scuttled into a corner (or whatever you call the edge of a hole that gives shelter), pulled some sand over herself, and waited for the killing sun to fall into the ocean one more time. What she would do after that, she had no idea.

And she was starving.

She was dying and she was *starving*.

Okay: She was *dead* and she was starving.

From above: "Hey."

She said nothing.

"Hey. Down there." Pause. "In the hole."

She couldn't resist, could not physically prevent her jaw from opening and the nagging voice from bursting forth, it was just so exquisitely *stupid*, that question: "What, down the hole? Where else would I be? Dumb shit."

Longer pause. "I'll, uh, get help."

"Don't do that. I'll be fine."

"Someone'll have some rope in their truck."

"Why don't you have rope in your truck?" she couldn't resist asking.

"Don't need it."

It was amazing: the man (nice voice—deep, calm, almost bored) sounded as indifferent as a . . . a—she couldn't think of what.

"I don't, either."

"Don't either what?"

Nice voice: not too bright. "Don't need a rope. I do not need a rope. No rope!" No, indeed! A rescue right now would be disastrous. She could picture it with awful clarity: heave

and heave, and here she is, thank goodness she's safe, and
what the hell? She's on—She's on *fire!*

As her hero, Homer Simpson, would have said: "D'oh!"

"How did you even fall in there?" her would-be rescuer
was asking. "It's impossible for there to be a deep hole on the
beach. The sand would fill it up."

"I'm not a marine biologist, okay?" she snapped.

"Geologist," he suggested. "You're not a geologist."

It was amazing: she'd spent the day alone, in hours of
silence, terrified of the sunlight, hoping she wouldn't face an
ugly death, and now she wanted her rescuer to get the hell
lost.

"Get the hell lost."

Pause. "Did you hit your head on the way down?"

"On *what?*"

"You seem," he added, "kind of unpleasant."

"I'm in a *hole.*"

"Well. I can't just leave you there."

"Oh, sure you can," she encouraged. "Just . . . keep going
to wherever you were going."

"I didn't really have anywhere to go."

"Oh, boo friggin' hoo. Is this the part where I go all dewy
between my legs and talk about how I'm secretly lonely, too,
and how it was meant to be, me falling on my ass and you
hauling me out? And then we Do It?"

"Did someone push you down there?"

"Shut up and go away. I'll be fine."

"Maybe the fire department?" he mused aloud.

"No. No. No no no no no no."

"Well. You can't exactly stop me."

She gasped. "You wouldn't *dare*."

"Even if you are crazy. I can't just not help you."

"Go away, Boy Scout."

"It's just that I can't hang around too much longer."

"Great. Fine. Have a good time, wherever you're going. See ya."

"I have this thing."

"Okeydokey!" she said brightly, her inner Minnesotan coming out, which was an improvement over her inner cannibal, which wanted to choke and eat this mystery man, claw strips of flesh from his bones and strangle him with them, then poke a hole in his jugular and drink him down like a blue raspberry Slushee Pup. "Bye-bye then!"

"But I could maybe keep you company until it's time to . . . for me to go." Another pause, then, in a lower voice: "Although that might not work, either."

"Aw, no," she almost groaned. "You're going to talk down my hole, then go away?"

"Yeah, you're right. That won't work."

"For more reasons than you can figure, Boy Scout."

"I don't have a cell phone, is the thing."

"Me neither. Aw, that's so sweet, look how much we have in common; too bad we're not having sex right this second."

Pause. "You keep bringing up sex."

"Yeah, well. It's been a long fargin' day."

"Fargin'?"

"Shut up, Boy Scout."

"It's just that you don't have to worry."

"That's a humungous load off my mind, Boy Scout."

"Because the thing is, I can't . . . you don't have . . . it's that I'm not attracted to you at all."

She clutched her head. "This. Is. Not. Happening."

"I don't mean to hurt your feelings."

Insanely, he had. "Hey up there! For all you know, I'm an anorexic blonde with huge tits, skin the color of milk, and a case of raging nymphomania."

Another of those maddening pauses. "Anyway, that's not really the problem. The problem—"

"Bud. I so don't need you to tell me what the problem is. Please get lost."

She heard a sudden intake of breath, as if he'd come to a quick, difficult decision, and then there was a *whoosh* and a *thud*, and he was standing next to her.

Chapter 3

Five minutes later she was still screaming at him. *Right* at him. The hole was only about three feet in diameter. They were chest to chest. And she was loud. Really loud.

". . . left your *brains* up there, Boy Scout, not that you ever were that *heavy* in the smarts department in the *first* place!"

"It just seemed like a good idea, is all."

"Seemed like a good idea?"

"Wow. You're really loud. While you're yelling, I'll make a step, and throw you out."

"You'll make a what and what me what?"

"Make a step with my hands. Like this." He bent forward to show her, and they promptly bonked skulls.

"Ow!"

He could feel himself get red. "Sorry." And red wasn't the

only thing he was getting. What had he been thinking? She was right: he'd left his brains up there with the seagull shit.

"This was your solution?" she scolded, rubbing her forehead. "No cell phone, no rope, and now we're *both* down here?"

"It's really small down here," he said, trying not to sound tense. "It didn't look that small from up top."

"It's a hole, Boy Scout. Not a cavernous underground lair."

He scratched his arm, and when his elbow knocked against the side of the hole, sand showered down, which made him itch more.

"Can you breathe okay?" He tried not to gasp. "Is there enough air down here? I don't think there's enough air down here."

"Oh boy oh boy. I am not believing this. You actually took a terrible situation, made it worse, then made it *more* worse. Are you all right?"

"It's just that there's no air down here." He clutched his head. "None at all."

"You're claustrophobic and you jumped down into a hole?"

He groaned. "Don't talk about it."

"But why, Boy Scout?"

"Couldn't just leave you here. But you're not really here." He sniffed hard. Her hair was a perfect cap of dark curls (he thought; there wasn't much light down here), and under normal circumstances he would find that extremely cute. He sniffed her head again. "I don't think you're here at all."

"Boy Scout, you have lost what little tiny cracker brains you had to begin with." She managed to fold her arms over her chest and (he thought) glare at him. "If this is some elaborate ploy to impress me in order to get laid—"

"I can't have sex with you. You're not here." He gasped again. "I can't breathe. How can you breathe?"

"Well, apparently I'm not here," she said dryly. "And don't get me started on why the whole oxygen thing isn't a problem for me. I— What are you doing?"

He stumbled around and was scrabbling at the sandy walls, digging for purchase and doing nothing but pulling a shower of sand down on them both.

"Boy Scout, get a grip!" She coughed and spat a few grains of sand at his back. "You're just making it worse!"

She was yammering at his back and he didn't hear, couldn't hear, sand was everywhere, in his mouth, in his ears, in his eyes, and it was so close, it wasn't a hole, it was a grave and it was filling up, filling up with him in it.

He clawed at the wall, pulled, yanked, scrabbled, tried to climb, and he could hear the woman yelling, screaming, feel her blows on his shoulders and they were as heavy as flies landing.

Then the moon was there. The moon came for him in the grave and took him out, took him up and out, and he was able to gouge himself out of the grave with two ungainly leaps and then he was screaming, screaming at the moon, howling at the moon, and she wasn't screaming anymore, the grave was full and she was quiet, at last she was quiet and he ran, ran, ran with the moon and his last thought as a man was, "What have I done?"

Chapter 2

"It's around here," Burke said, so ashamed he couldn't look up from the sand.

"Around here?" Jeannie Wyndham, his pack's female Alpha, poked at the small dunes with a sneakered toe. "That's pretty vague for a guy with a nose like yours. Is this the spot or isn't it?"

"I . . . think it is. It's hard to tell. I can't smell her at all. I can just smell me. And I'm all over the place. After I got out of the gra—hole, I just ran."

Michael, his pack leader, was crouched and balanced on the balls of his feet as his yellow gaze swept the area. He said nothing, for which Burke was profoundly grateful. He couldn't have borne a scolding, as much as he deserved one.

"Burke, give us a break," Jeannie said, sounding (no surprise at all) exasperated. "You stumbled across a woman who needed help—"

"And I left her to die."

"—and you did what you could. You guys are— Every werewolf I've ever *met* is such a screaming claustrophobe you should all be on tranqs, but you jumped into a hole to try to save her before you Changed. She didn't have a chance in hell anyway."

Burke could think of several chances the poor dead woman might have had, but it wasn't prudent to correct Jeannie, so he stayed silent.

"There, I think," Michael said. There was a deep depression in the sand, a jumble of footprints—and wolf tracks, leading away. "You're right, Burke. I can smell you all over the sand, and a few other people—tourists who just came out for the day, people just passing by—and that's it. Certainly there's no scent of a woman who'd been trapped in the bottom of a hole for over twenty hours."

"Well, if you can't smell her, and Burke can't smell her . . ." Jeannie trailed off, then mumbled, "He needs a girlfriend."

"I'm not making it up."

"Of course not," Michael said with a hard look at his wife. She stuck her tongue out at him, and he continued. "But there have been, ah, concerns. You've lived alone most of your life. No one sees you. The only time any of us see you is if I summon you—God knows I don't do that unless it's a real emergency, or to meet a new baby—"

Burke didn't say anything, but he knew where Michael was

going. Werewolves were *not* solitary creatures. They were designed to mate young and drop lots of pups. Rogues—even gentle ones—made everyone nervous. Now they thought that the stress of never having children had driven him over the edge. If he hadn't been so miserably ashamed, he would have laughed.

"At least yesterday was the last night of the full moon," Jeannie said, shading her eyes as she watched the sun dip into the ocean. "Or there'd be no talking to either of you in another five minutes."

"I came back to the mansion as soon as I could," Burke explained. "When I woke up this morning, I was in Vermont." No surprise. He had run and run and run, but had never managed to leave his shame and guilt and horror behind.

"Well, no one's around. Why don't we do a little digging and see what, uh, comes up?" Jeannie asked with *faux* brightness.

Burke knew, as did Michael, that despite the deepening gloom there *were* people around, but no one was close. And in any case, digging holes in the beach wasn't exactly suspicious behavior. Hell, people paid money for clamming licenses *just* to dig at the beach.

He dropped to all fours and began to scoop out great handfuls of sand with his hands, ignoring the shovels Jeannie had brought.

"Cheer up," Jeannie said, shifting her weight uncomfortably from foot to foot. "There probably isn't anybody—I mean, we might not find anything."

"And if we do find anything, it wasn't your fault."

"Excuse me," Burke said politely, "but it was *entirely* my fault. I appreciate you coming out here with me."

"Like we're going to let you dig around in the dark by yourself, thinking you'll stumble across a corpse? Yuck, Burke! Besides, the whole thing's a joke. You're only the nicest, gentlest, quietest werewolf out there. You'd no more kill a woman than I'd break Lara's arm."

"Not that she couldn't use that sort of thing," Michael said shortly; he was saving his breath for digging.

Burke grunted and kept digging. He knew Lara, a charming creature and the future pack leader, and frankly, he wondered how Jeannie had *kept* from breaking the high-spirited girl's arm. The cub wasn't even in her teens yet, and some of her exploits were already legendary, like the time she jumped off the roof of the mansion and used her quilt as a parachute; except it hadn't worked out quite the way she planned and she'd come down like a stone, breaking one ankle and scaring the holy old shit out of her parents.

Heh. That had been a day.

"How long—are we—going to dig—before we decide—Burke isn't a killer?" Jeannie panted.

"Until we find the—" Burke froze, reached deeper, and felt his fingers closing around . . . a forearm. He leaned back and pulled, tears stinging his eyes from the sand. Yeah, the sand and the thought of that poor woman dying alone, dying in the dark, dying as the sand filled her nose and lungs and finally stopped her heart.

Dying alone.

"Oh my God!" Jeannie screamed in a whisper as he stood,

pulling the body free from the sand until it was dangling from his strong grip like a puppet whose strings had been cut. "Burke! Oh my God!"

"You— I guess we'd better try to find her family," Michael said, recovering quickly, which was why he was the boss and Burke was the Clam Cop. "If we can't, we'll give her a proper—"

"Oh no you *don't*!" the body snapped, swinging in the air and kicking Burke in the shin. "You didn't dig me up just to plop me into another grave. And *you*," she snarled, as sand showered from her hair, her face, fell from her shoulders and her clothes and fangs—*fangs?*—and hit the beach. "I'm starving and it's all—your—fault!" So saying, she lunged forward, fastened to Burke's shoulders like a lamprey, and sank her teeth into the side of his neck.

Chapter 5

It took the combined strength of Jeannie and Michael, plus a lot of tugging and yelling and threatening, before the dead woman was pulled off. Everyone was scratched and bleeding before it was over.

"Don't talk to me," the dead woman said, wiping the blood off her chin and backing away from them. "Don't talk to me, don't look at me, don't bury me."

"But . . . you . . ." Jeannie groped for the words and ended up waving her arms in the air like a cheerleader who'd forgotten her routine. "You can't . . . you . . ."

Michael cleared his throat. "Ma'am, you're dead. You have no scent, you have no pulse. You, uh, should lie down and be dead."

"Aw, shut the hell up." She whirled and pointed a dirty finger at Burke, who had been trying to figure out if he was terrified or relieved. "And you! The number of your gross offenses against me grows by the hour! The *half* hour! Now leave. Me. Alone!"

She whirled and stomped away, her fists clenching as she heard all three of them hurry after her.

She turned back. "Leave. Me. Alone. Any of that unclear? Any of you not speak such good English?"

"I get it!" Jeannie cried with the hysterical good humor of a *Jeopardy!* contestant. "You're a vampire!"

"No, she isn't," Burke and Michael said in unison.

The body stomped her foot, and all three of them took a step back. "Of course I'm a vampire, morons! What else would I be? A Sasquatch? Nessie?"

"There are no such thing as vampires," Michael said gently. "I think you must have gone into shock when you were buried and that protected you until we could rescue you—"

"*Rescue* me?"

"And the whole thing has been too much for your system and now you think—"

"Oh, what crap. I don't need to breathe, *ergo*, I didn't suffocate, and I couldn't get out of the hole during the day. *Ergo*, I wasn't buried alive. Are you honestly telling me that werewolves don't believe in vampires?"

"The existence of one doesn't prove the other," Michael said stiffly. "I believe in witches, but that doesn't mean I believe in leprechauns."

"How'd you know they were werewolves?" Jeannie asked, examining the scratch on her left elbow.

"Because Boy Scout lost all his little tiny marbles, went

into a screaming fit worthy of a Beatles fan, turned into a wolf, and jumped out of a twelve-foot hole. Call me crazy."

"Crazy," Jeannie said brightly.

Burke touched the bite mark on his neck, which was already scabbing over. It would explain a lot: her relative calm at being in such a fix, her utter lack of scent, and, of course, her walking and talking after being buried alive for more than twenty-four hours.

All his life, he had been told legends of wolves and fairies and water witches, and a grizzled beta had once claimed to have seen a demon, but never had he heard of a vampire, or even seen one.

Until, obviously, now.

"You're alive," he said, and it was impossible to keep the relief out of his voice, though he tried. Despite his efforts, both Jeannie and Michael turned and gave him odd looks.

"Newsflash, Boy Scout: I've been dead for forty years. Sorry about the . . . you know—" She gestured vaguely in their direction: all three were scratched, bitten, disheveled, sandy. "I was hungry and the thirst got a little away from me. Now, I gotta go. I'd eat a rat just for the chance to have a hot shower."

Without another word, she turned and moved off into the dunes.

Burke looked at his pack leaders. "Good-bye," he said simply.

Michael stuck out his hand and they shook. "I guess we won't be seeing you for a while. If ever."

"What?" Jeannie asked.

"I don't know," he replied honestly. "I guess it's up to . . . to . . . I don't even know her name."

"We'll keep your house for you. Everything that's yours will always be here for you."

"What?" Jeannie asked again.

"Thank you, Michael. I appreciate your help tonight. Do I have your leave to go?"

"You have my leave, O brother, and good hunting and many cubs," he replied, the formal good-bye of a pack leader releasing a beta male from his care.

"You're going after her? You've decided you're going to be mates and live happily ever after even though she's dead and you don't even know her name?"

"Good-bye, Jeannie."

"Burke!" she yowled, but he ignored her and loped off into the dark, a true rogue, now.

Chapter 6

Somehow, Boy Scout had flanked her, because he was waiting for her in the parking lot, the fluorescent lights bouncing off his black hair, making it seem very like the color of blood.

"I have a shower," he said by way of greeting.

"One side, Boy Scout. I've seen all of you I'm gonna."

"And a house. You could stay there and . . . and rest during the day and do your business at night."

Hmm. Tempting. Credit cards could be traced, a decent hotel wouldn't take cash, and she didn't want anyone to see her coming and going. Shacking up with a stranger for a night or two was— Wait. Had she lost her mind? Because she was actually mulling it over. Crazy guy's offer. As if he hadn't left her in the biggest fix of her life just last night.

Well. Second biggest.

Although, her gentler self argued, he had tried to help her. Badly, but the effort counted for something, right?

"Please," he said, and that did it. She was undone; it wasn't the "please," it was how he looked when he said it: miserable and hopeful all at once.

"Oh, all right," she grumbled. "Maybe for the night. I hope one of these cars is yours."

"It's not. But my house is just over the dunes, past the Beachside Motel." He pointed at a row of lights in the distance, and she sighed internally. It had been a rough couple of nights, and she wasn't up to a hike, undead strength or not.

She opened her mouth to bitch, only to feel herself be swept off the warm pavement and into his arms. "It's not far," he promised her, and went loping through the lot and into the dunes.

"Boy Scout, you're gonna break your fargin' back!" she hollered, secretly delighted. When was the last time she had been picked up and carried like a bride over the threshold? Her mama had died when she was a toddler; her dad was too busy working two jobs to pick her up; cancer had taken him her first year at the U of M. After that . . . "I weigh a ton!"

"Hardly," he said, and the sly mother wasn't even out of breath. He raced with her across the sand, past the motel, up a small hill covered with stumpy, stubbly bushes, and then he was setting her down on a sandy porch. She turned and looked, and could barely make out the lights of the parking lot. Boy Scout could *move*. But then, she'd seen evidence of that just the night before.

He opened the door and made an odd gesture—half wave, half bow.

She walked into the house. "No locks, huh? Doncha just love the Cape."

"No one would dare," he said simply. "Will the lights hurt your eyes? We can leave them off if you prefer."

"No, the lights are fine."

Click.

They blinked at each other in his living room, both getting their first good look at the other, and both entirely pleased by what they saw.

For her part, she saw a tall, thin, black-haired man with gray eyes—the only gray eyes she'd ever seen, true gray, the color of the sky when it was about to storm. He was dressed in dirty shorts, shirtless and barefoot, and as tanned as an old shoe. Laugh lines—except he never laughed, or smiled—around those amazing, storm-colored eyes. His legs were ropy with muscle and his arms looked like a swimmer's: lean and strong. His hands were large and capable-looking. His mouth was a permanent downturned bow; even when he tried to smile, he looked like he was frowning. She liked it, being in a generally bad mood herself; sometimes it was nice to be away from perpetual smilers, and Minnesota had more than its fair share.

Burke saw a tall woman (she came up to his chin in her bare feet) with a classically beautiful face, strong nose, wide forehead, pointed chin. Black eyes, skin the color of espresso. Long, slim limbs. Wide shoulders that made her breasts almost disappear. Unpainted toes and fingernails; filthy linen pants and a T-shirt so dirty he had no idea what the original color was. And if he closed his eyes he couldn't see her: she gave off no scent of her own, only sand and sea. She was like a chameleon for the nose; she took on the smells around her, the smells he loved. He thought her accent was the same way: she didn't sound like much of anything. She didn't drop her R's like the locals, had no Midwestern twang, no Southern drawl. She didn't sound like anything. Or, rather, she sounded like just herself, and that was exactly right.

And there it was: that sense of rightness about her, the sense that she was for him and he was for her. Even though only one of them knew it.

That was all right. He was a patient man.

She mistook his silence for something else and glanced down at herself, the first time he had seen her self-conscious: "Ugh, look at me. I must stink as bad as I look."

"You're beautiful."

"Ugh, stop it right now."

"But you are," he said, puzzled.

Her brown eyes narrowed as she studied him. "Boy Scout, get those thoughts out of your head right this minute."

"Thoughts that you're beautiful?"

"Uh-huh. I'm not beautiful; it's the vampire mystique. It's like . . . like a hormone I give off. Makes it easier for me to bite you. Any vampire can do it."

"You don't smell like anything; how can you be giving off a hormone?"

"Because, trust me, I'm not beautiful. I've got a big nose and big feet and tiny tits and my hair never grows so I always look like a shorn sheep."

He was dizzy with the wrongness of her self-perception. "Huh?"

"This will never work out. Not in a thousand years."

"Huh?"

"Look at us."

He smiled.

"No, really look."

"I don't care that you're a vampire."

"You don't even know what a vampire is, or does."

"So? You'll show me."

"And the age difference?"

He shrugged.

"Boy Scout, I've got at least fifty years on you! I was thirty when I died!"

"So call a nursing home."

"And . . ."

"And?"

"You're white."

He waited for the rest of the explanation, and she had to resist the urge to put her fist through his television set. "I'm black, you're white. Are you listening?"

"You mean— You're a bigot?"

"*I'm* not! Everybody else is! And don't even tell me how trendy it is to be black or to have a black girlfriend because trends are cyclical, they are, and one day you'll wake up and I won't be trendy and then where will we be?"

"Miss," he said patiently, "do you want that shower or not?"

"Boy Scout, you're not hearing a thing I'm saying, are you?"

"You have eyes like chocolate," he said dreamily.

"You don't even know my name."

"Oh. Well. Mine's Burke Wolftaur."

"Of course it is. Great disguise, by the way, werewolf. Running around on the beach right before a full moon, got the word *wolf* in your damned last name, *real* bright."

He shrugged. "I was on my way back to my house; I would have made it in plenty of time if I hadn't run into you."

"Oh, so it's *my* fault you're a dumbass?"

"Yes. And all the packs' names go back to the same roots. There are hundreds of Wolfs, Wolftons, Wolfbauers, Wolfertons, right here on the Cape."

"I repeat: great disguise, dumbass. I'm Serena Crull, by the way."

"Cruel?" he asked.

"C-R-U-L-L."

"Oh."

"Well, at least my name isn't Serena Vampireton, ya big putz."

"The bathroom is down the hall and on your left. I'll find some clean clothes for you."

"Had lots of lady friends stay over, hum?"

"No, you'll have to make do with my clothes."

"Ah, let the fashion show begin!"

"You'll be lovely," he said flatly, as if stating a fact: It will rain tonight. It was too cloudy to stargaze. You will be lovely.

"Boy Scout, you are one weird white boy, anybody tell you?"

"Never to my face," he replied, and went to find her something to wear.

Chapter 7

Burke shut the fridge and turned around, then nearly dropped the gallon of milk on his foot. Serena was standing *right there* and he hadn't heard a thing.

"That's disconcerting."

"Thanks, Boy Scout. If that's for me, don't bother. I don't drink . . . milk."

"It's for me, actually. I can still taste the sand from last night." He poured himself a large glass and drank it all off in a single draught, like it was beer. He could use a beer, but there wasn't a drop in the house. He scowled at the gallon container, then poured himself more.

"How are you feeling?" he asked.

"I was about to ask you the same thing." She grabbed a napkin from the small pile on the kitchen table, stepped forward, and wiped his upper lip. "I can't hardly see where I bit you anymore."

"Fast healer. Fast metabolism."

"Honey, tell me." She stepped back—almost too quickly, he thought, as if she was afraid. Not that he could exactly tell—it was maddening not to be able to smell her emotions. And tantalizing. But mostly maddening. "So?" She whirled in a small circle. "How do I look? Ready to call *Vogue*?"

"You look fine," he said, which was a gross underestimation. She was wearing one of his white strappy T-shirts, which only emphasized her small, firm breasts and the sweet dark smoothness of her skin. Frankly, the shirt emphasized that her breasts were all nipple, which made him want to pull it off to see, which made him want to—

"Fine," he repeated, wrenching his mind back on track. Trying, anyway. "You look fine."

"Well, the sweatpants were never gonna work, so I found a pair of your shorts." As it was, they came down to her knees and made her look irresistibly cute; she wiggled her bare toes and he smiled. She was still damp from the shower; water glistened in her tight cap of black curls.

He hurriedly drank more milk. Pity that wasn't what he was thirsty for.

"Well, I appreciate the clothes and the shower and the late-night snack—" She tapped her throat by explanation and he nodded. "But I'd better hit the trail, as they said in the old Westerns right before they killed all the Indians. Excuse me: Native Americans."

"Hold on. I want to help you."

"Help me out of these shorts, maybe," she joked, and he hurriedly looked away so she wouldn't realize how close she was to the truth. "Naw, I think we've bugged each other enough for one night—well, two nights. Don't you?"

"You can't do it by yourself."

"Do what?"

"Whatever it is you came here for. You're not a native, and you're not a tourist. Something brought you to the Cape. I want to help you with it."

"Why?"

Because you're beautiful. Because I was a coward. Because you know what I am and you're not afraid. Because I know what you are and I'm not afraid. Because. Because.

"I feel bad," he said carefully, "about last night."

She waved his cowardice away with one nail-bitten hand. "That? Forget it."

"Never."

She raised her eyebrows at his tone. "I mean it. I made a fuss, but it was no big. It was sweet—yet dumb—of you to jump in at all. You couldn't help your nature, any more than I can help biting people on the neck. And I quit apologizing for *that* about thirty years ago."

"Still, you're rogue." *Like me.*

"Rogue?"

"Out here by yourself. Alone. You don't have the pack to help you. But I'll help you."

"Boy Scout, I really don't think you will."

"On my word as a former member of the Wyndham Pack, I will."

"Boy Scout, you don't want any of this, trust me."

"I left you once and it almost killed you."

She snorted. "Not even close."

"I can't leave you again. At least—" He groped for a way to lighten the moment, make a joke. What would a real person *say*? "At least not until we get you some decent clothes."

"You're sweet, but you shouldn't offer to jump into something when you don't know what it is."

Patiently, he went over it again. "I don't care what it is. I want to help you. Frankly, I don't see you leaving this house without me right behind you. I'm an excellent tracker." A bluff, with her lack of scent, she could probably lose him in half an hour.

She scowled, then shrugged. "Have it your way, Boy Scout. You rang the cherries: I'm not a tourist. I'm out here for a reason. In fact, I'm out here to find a vampire and kill him. How 'bout that?"

"Oh, murder? That's fine with me."

To his amusement, she was so shocked she sat down.

Chapter 8

"See, the thing is—"

"It's fine, Serena."

"But see, it's like—"

"Do you want to leave now? Or do you need to, I don't know, rest?"

"Listen to me. I . . . we . . . have to find the vampire who—"

"Who sired you?"

She made a face, her dark nose crinkling like she smelled something bad. Since he hadn't taken the garbage out for a day or two, it was entirely possible. Perhaps they shouldn't be having this meeting in the kitchen. Perhaps another room. Like the bedroom. Ah, the—

"Boy Scout, you're not listening. Nobody says 'sired'; a vampire makes you or he kills you. In fact, a lot of us say we were killed, even *if* we were made. Are you— Was that a yawn?"

"I haven't been sleeping."

"It *was* a yawn! What, I'm boring you?"

"I'm just not interested in the details."

"The details like who we're going to murder."

"According to you," he said coolly, "our victim is already dead."

That gave her something to think about, he could see; she leaned back in her kitchen chair and stared up at the ceiling for a minute. Finally she brushed her ear—a charming monkey gesture—and said, "Well, okay. Technically, the guy we're going to stake doesn't breathe and doesn't have a pulse, or not much of one, and he's been running around dead for at least sixty years. But still. It's a very serious thing."

Burke managed to conceal another yawn.

"I can't believe," she said, shaking her head, "that you don't at least want the details."

"Oh, sure, I want them. Who, when, and how, I suppose. He's probably going to be a hard kill." He smiled and Serena shrank back in her chair. "You certainly were."

"Okay, first of all, when you grin like that, you've got about a million teeth. Second of all, the *who* is the vampire who made me, yeah. The *when* is as soon as I track the mother down, and the *how*—we have to stake him in the heart or throw him into a tanning bed or something like that."

"Crosses? Holy water?"

"Will hurt him but probably not kill him. And don't be waving any of those things around *me*, Boy Scout."

"Does the stake have to be made of—"

"Any kind of wood. And it has to be through the heart. Anywhere else, he'll just get right back up and keep coming." She added bitterly, "Don't ask me how I know this."

Burke ground his teeth. "Did he hurt you?"

"Huh? No. I mean . . . not physically."

"But you want him dead for making you dead."

"No. For making my friend dead. I want him dead for lying. He *lied*. He didn't tell me the truth. I mean the whole truth. He let me believe that whoever he bit would be a vampire. He didn't tell me . . . didn't—" She covered her face with her hands and went silent.

After a minute, Burke said, "He bit you."

"Yes."

"And you came back."

"Yes."

"You were lonely."

Serena's hands came down; her eyes were big with wonder. "Yes. Once the hunger—the being new, the being crazy of a new vampire—once that wore off, I found my friend. My best and greatest friend, Maggie Dunn."

"She missed you."

"She was so *happy* that I was alive. Sort of alive. You know. And—"

"You talked to your friend. Or Maggie asked you. It doesn't matter."

"That's right," she choked. "It doesn't matter."

"You thought, or she thought, being a vampire would be a fine thing. Friends forever. And your sire—the one who made

you—he obliged. He didn't tell you—what? Did he not per-
form all the rituals? Did he do it wrong out of spite, or to keep
his pack's numbers down?"

"He didn't tell me, and I only found out later, that being a
vampire . . . it's like the measles. It's something you catch. Or
don't catch. You could get bit by the same vampire a hundred
times, and ninety-nine of those times, nothing would happen.
Or he'd drink too much and you'd die. But that one time, the
hundredth time, you'd come back. I thought—I didn't know
it was a fargin' *virus*. I didn't know it was a damned head cold.
And he didn't tell me. Didn't warn us."

"Your friend didn't come back."

"My friend." She took a shuddering breath and obviously wasn't used to it, because she almost tilted off her chair
and onto the floor. "My friend died screaming. And I let it
happen."

"And this was . . ."

"Nineteen sixty-five." She smiled. It was a wobbly smile,
but it was there. "Free love, you know."

"Why . . . now?"

"I finally found him, that's why now. There's a new regime
in place, and the king helped me track him down."

He blinked, processing this. "The king."

"King Sinclair. The king of the vampires. He made the
Minneapolis librarian track Peter down for me."

"Peter?"

"Innocuous name for such a scum-sucking son of a bitch,
isn't it? Anyway, the old boss didn't give two shits for prob-
lems like mine. I knew better than to even ask—we all just

kept out of his way. It was a bad time for most of us. But then—"

"Things changed."

"I heard the new king and queen—"

"There was a coup for power? The old leader lost? Was killed?"

"Yeah. So I let things settle down a bit and then I went to St. Paul and— Never mind all that, point is, I got an address, I even got the name of the restaurant he runs."

"Your leaders—they know what you'll do when you find Peter?"

She nibbled on her lower lip. "The king does. He understands this kind of stuff. I got the feeling—I think he keeps the queen out of a lot of the bloodier stuff, you know? She's kind of new to the game."

"Ah." He knew about new mates, having seen (from a distance) Jeannie's struggles to fit in with the pack. He didn't blame this Sinclair fellow at all for keeping his woman out of the boring bloody details.

"That's it? 'Ah'?"

"There is nothing else, right?"

"Yeah, but . . . that's it? You got nothin'?"

"Do you know what my mother told me every night before I went to bed?"

"Uh . . . stop being such a chowderhead?"

"No. She repeated the family motto: Kill or be eaten."

"Swell."

"Isn't that your situation, as a vampire?"

She shifted in her chair. "I-I don't think of myself—I

mean, I don't think I've ever killed anyone. It's a myth that vampires have to kill you to feed. Half a pint and we're good for the night. Sure, we're a little bit nuts in the beginning—a brand-new vampire is pretty much out of her mind for a few years. But you get ahold. It's like anything—you deal."

He touched his neck, which had entirely healed, and smiled at her. "Good to know."

"But it sounds like being a werewolf is really, really stressful. No wonder you live away from it all."

"That's not why I live away from it all," he said, and got up to put the milk away, and they both knew the discussion was over.

Chapter 9

Before she realized it, the night had disappeared and the killing dawn was lurking around the corner. Serena could hardly believe it. They'd spent the entire night in the kitchen, plotting.

Born and bred on the Cape, Burke knew the local geography and tourist traps, and recognized the name of Pete's restaurant, Eat Me Raw. He told her it was "up Cape" in "P-town," whatever the hell that meant. Not for the first time, she thought it wasn't so crazy, hooking up with the Boy Scout.

"We could drive there now," he said, looking at her doubtfully, "but you'd have to ride in the trunk. And stay in the trunk until the sun goes down."

"Tempting offer, but no thanks. Let's just crash here and we'll hit the road first thing tonight. You've got a whole day," she teased, "to come to your senses."

Without a word, he got up and escorted her to the basement of his small, pleasantly untidy house. It was a finished basement, cool and dark, partly used for storage. Part of the basement had been made into a bedroom, with one small south-facing window, which he efficiently taped a dark beach towel over.

"All rightey then," she said, looking at the neatly made double bed. The room screamed "guest room"; there was no personality to it at all. In fact, Burke's entire house (well, the parts she had seen) had very little personality, as if occupied by a ghost, or someone who didn't care much one way or the other. "Good night."

"Good night." He stood very close to her for a moment and then (she thought—hoped?) reluctantly moved away. "Call me if you need anything."

"Oh yeah. You betcha." She cursed her Minnesotaisms, which surfaced in moments of stress.

The door shut. She was alone in the sterile guest room. Which was too bad, because she hadn't been laid in about twenty years (the thirst tended to take over everything, including the sex drive and the need for manicures) and Burke would obviously be a—

But that was no way to think. That way was trouble, pure and simple. She had a mission to complete, and when Pete was dead, when his lying head had been cut off and she'd kicked it into the ocean, when Maggie had at long last been avenged, then . . . then . . .

Well. She didn't know. But that was for later. For now, she climbed between clean sheets and, when the sun came up (she couldn't see it, but she could sure feel it, feel it the way bats felt it, the way blind worms in the dirt felt it), she slept.

And dreamed.

This was delightful, as it hadn't happened often. She hadn't known vampires could dream at all until it started happening to her about five years ago.

In her dream (wonderful dream, delightful dream) she and Maggie (Maggie!) were walking around in Dinkytown, just a few blocks away from the apartment they'd shared as college students. It was the fifties, and they both wore black capris and white men's shirts tied around their twenty-year-old midriffs. Maggie wore ballet flats on her little delicate feet (oh, how she'd envied Maggie her feet), and Serena wore saddle shoes, which were the slightest bit too tight, but who cared? The sun was shining and oh, it was good to be young and alive and eating ice cream cones and welcoming the admiring glances from the fellows on the sidewalk in June, in Minnesota, in summer, in life.

"Place has twenty flavors of homemade ice cream, glorious hand-cranked ice cream like Grandma makes, and you always pick vanilla." Serena took another bite of coconut chip and tried not to look smug.

"Never mind my choices, let's talk about yours. You've given up happiness for how many decades, and for what? To avenge me? For what? Because you feel guilty?"

The ice cream suddenly tasted like ashes, and Serena had to fight the urge to spit out the bite. "I don't want to talk about that now. This is supposed to be a nice damned dream."

"Tough noogies, chowderhead." Maggie brushed her

bangs out of her eyes and Serena noticed the ragged bite marks—chew marks—all around her friend's neck. Something had been at her, and hadn't been nice about it, either. "You managed to literally stumble into some happiness, and what? Did you jump on him and try to make a baby?"

"I can't have—"

"Or did you drag him down into your sick old shit?"

"Maggie, he has to pay!"

They both knew the "he" Serena was talking about. "Sure he does. But do you?"

"I don't know what you—"

"You never did, honey. That's why I'm the scholarship student, and you're running around dead on Cape Cod. No lover, no home, no nothing. Just your bad old self. And for what?"

"Maggie, I can hear you *screaming* in my *sleep*. Vampires don't even dream and most of the time I dream about *that*."

"That's on you, honeygirl." Her friend looked at her with terrible affection, the vanilla melting in her fist, the blood running down her blouse front. "You didn't want to spend eternity alone; who would? So here we are, both dead. But now you've got another chance—and you're wrecking that one, too. The first time was piss-ignorance. Not your fault. But this? Willful."

"It's not—"

"Well, you always were the stubborn one." Her friend grinned, all teeth and gums and blood. "And I was the pretty one."

"Maggie—"

"See you 'round, honeygirl."

Maggie vanished. The stores vanished. The old-fashioned (at least, to her twenty-first-century eyes) cars vanished. The sidewalk patrons vanished. There was only her, and her stupid coconut chip ice cream cone, and her too-tight saddle shoes, and—

—the guest bedroom.

It was night again and the thirst was on her; her mouth felt like dust, her mouth felt dead. Dead. Like Maggie, long dirt and bones in her lonely grave. The grave Serena had helped put her in. Had *led* her to.

She shoved back the blanket and was on her feet, then up the stairs and headed for the door. She had to drink before she could think, and she certainly wasn't going to chomp Burke again, poor boy. She had enough guilt on her shoulders without—

"Where are you going?"

"Don't sneak up on me, Boy Scout," she said without turning around. "Bad habit."

"But where are you going?"

"Breakfast. Well, supper. Can't say when I'll be back."

She hadn't heard him cross the room, but suddenly his arm closed over her elbow. "Rules of the house," he said simply, looking down at her with his storm-colored eyes. "You have to eat what the host serves." He tugged the neck of his T-shirt down, exposing his jugular. "Me."

Chapter 10

In a perfect world, she would have logically reasoned out why it wasn't appropriate to bite the boy, the infant—cripes, how old *was* he?

In a perfect world, she would have used her superior vampire strength to shake him off and gone traipsing down his porch and onto the beach, picked some drunken tourist and slaked her thirst, then come back and coolly discussed Pete's upcoming murder.

Neither she nor Burke lived in a perfect world; they yanked toward each other at the same moment (a clam between them would have shattered), mouths searching, tongues exploring, and then she reared back like the beast she was and bit him, pierced the vein with her teeth and sucked.

And nearly reeled; his blood was the richest, most satisfying drink she had ever had in all her years of being undead. In all her years, period. He tasted like salmon fighting upstream, like rabbits fucking under the moon, like wolves bringing down cattle.

They staggered around his living room in a rigid dance, fingers digging into each other's shoulders, and he pulled her (his, really) T-shirt off with one rip down the back. Not to be outdone by a mortal, she did the same. She hoped he had a stash of Clark Gable–type T-shirts somewhere, because he was now short two.

They tripped and hit the couch, Burke on the bottom, and she broke free and groaned at the ceiling. A bad idea with a full mouth; she caught a rill of blood with her thumb, then sucked on it.

"Good?" he asked.

"Burke. Oh man. You just don't know."

"It's my high-fat diet," he said seriously, staring at her tits. "Um. All nipples. Come here."

"Your high-fat diet includes nipples?"

"Shhh." His arm circled around her and he pulled her down, sucking greedily, even biting her gently, and she wriggled against him, pushing at her shorts, pulling at his.

She kissed the top of his head and shoved her breasts harder into his face, delighting in the feel of his mouth on her flesh. "Oh, Burke." She sighed.

"Mmmph."

"Not to put any pressure on you. But Reagan was in the White House the last time I got laid."

Her nipple slid from his mouth with a popping sound and he replied, "That's the opposite of pressure. It's been so long, you probably don't remember what good sex is."

"Come on!" she screeched, delighted. "It's like riding a bike."

"Hardly," he grunted, seizing her by the thighs and levering her over his mouth. She clutched the back of the sofa to keep her balance and promptly went out of her mind as his tongue searched, darted, stabbed. She couldn't imagine the upper-body strength he had, how he could so effortlessly hold her entire weight just above his mouth. The sheer physics of it was—was she thinking about physics?

Get your head in the game or you'll miss it. Good advice. Not to mention, she could feel his tongue all over, not just where . . . where it actually was. *Umm.* She shuddered all over and thrust against his face, no more able to stop her movements than she could have given up blood. And her orgasm was upon her like the finest rush imaginable, surging out of nowhere and shocking the shit out of her—she had never been one to come in less than five minutes, never mind less than five seconds.

She lost her grip but he did not, and the momentum brought them both tumbling to the floor, smashing the coffee table in three pieces on the way. Neither of them especially cared. They had one goal, and that was Serena's penetration: a shattered coffee table could not have been more irrelevant.

Burke crushed her lips beneath his mouth and shoved her legs apart with his knee; she locked her ankles behind his back as he pushed into her with no niceties and no apologies—just what she wanted, needed, silently demanded. Their bellies smacked together faster and faster, and they clawed and bit their way to mutual orgasm.

"Oh man," she said when she could talk.

"Hush."

"I'd fall down, if there was anywhere to fall."

"I knew you'd wreck this by speaking."

"Aw, shut it."

He brushed splinters out of her hair. "You owe me furniture."

"Ha! After that, you owe me a hundred bucks."

"Is that the going rate these days?"

"I have no idea," she admitted. "I just said that to sound tough." She was silent, considering. "I have no idea why I just said that, either."

"Well. You are tough." He gently disengaged from her limbs, picked her up like a doll and put her on the couch. He looked rueful as he examined the various shredded cloths that had been two outfits only five minutes ago, then said, "I'm ready for a burger or a steak or something. Are you—" He touched the bite wound on his neck. "Full?"

"Sure. Like I said before, we only need a little bit. But maybe you shouldn't be jumping around like that," she warned, getting up to put a hand on his arm—too late, he had already darted into the kitchen. "Sometimes vic—people are a little light-headed after I—"

He snorted, his head deep inside the fridge. "Eggs would be good. Eggs with a side of eggs. And a hamburger. Two hamburgers."

"I can hear your cholesterol going up, just listening." She was amazed at how energized he was. Werewolf, she reminded herself. All the time, not just during the full moon.

He brought down a bowl, rapidly cracked a dozen eggs into it, found a fork, and started whisking.

She came over to him and stared at the eggs. "Do you miss solid food?" he asked.

"No. The smell of it makes me ill. I can't believe you're going to eat half the food in the house."

He cocked a dark brow at her. "Half?"

"It's good that we got the sex out of the way," she said as they sped toward Eat Me Raw. "Now we can focus on—you know."

"The murder?"

"Right." She was a little taken aback at how coolly he said it, like it was a fact of life, something unpleasant but unavoidable, like taxes. "The sex thing would have just distracted you."

"That's probably true," he said cheerfully.

"But you know," she felt compelled to add, as she was compelled to ruin all good things in her life/death, "there's nothing in it for us. I mean, no future."

He was silent, concentrating on the road.

"It's not like I can give you a family. My ovaries quit working the same day everything quit working. Not that I ever wanted a family," she added in a mutter. "I hate kids."

"Me, too."

"Liar!"

He blinked at her. "Well. I don't *hate* them. I don't hate anything. But I must admit, they bug the shit out of me."

"Me, too! I mean, I know we all had to go through it, and kids have to learn, blah-blah, but do they have to learn right next to me? You can't go to a restaurant anywhere and have a nice glass of wine without some toddler throwing Saltines in your hair."

"And the parents . . ." he prompted.

"Oh, man, they are the *worst*! Always obsessing about when their kid takes a shit, or doesn't take a shit, or is a slow talker, or talks too much, and showing you meaningless crayon scribbles and going *on* and *on* about what geniuses their little Tommy or Jenny is. Ugh!"

"Try being in a pack, and knowing the baby barfing all over your shoes is destined to be your boss someday."

The sheer horror of the idea consumed her for a moment. "Okay," she said at last, "that's bad."

"Making nice to a toddler who takes a dump in the corner, because she's going to be the pack leader someday."

"Man!"

"And the parents, who are your bosses right now, think it's swell when the kid breaks a window by throwing her baby brother through it. So there's broken glass everywhere, the baby's laughing and shitting, the kid's laughing, and the parents are all 'isn't she a genius?' and 'isn't he a brave little man?'"

"I don't know how you stand it!"

"That's why I live alone. Lived alone," he corrected himself.

She let that pass. "Is it weird for a werewolf to not like kids?"

"Extremely. As in, perversion. We're supposed to be married by the time we can legally drink, and have two or three cubs by the time we're twenty-five."

She snickered at "cubs."

"But, I like my privacy. I like the beach. I like being able to sleep late on Saturdays and watch dirty movies on HBO whenever I want."

"Sing it."

She settled back in her seat and enjoyed the ride. He had an old pickup truck, beat-up blue with new tires and sprung upholstery. He had had it, he told her, for fifteen years.

Then she thought: I am riding in a blue truck with a near-stranger to go kill Pete, and I'm . . . happy?

Postcoital happiness, she decided. Strictly hormonal. She used to get the same high from eating chocolate.

"So, what's the plan?"

He blinked at her again. "You're asking me?"

"Okay. We go to the restaurant. We find Pete. We take him out back and kill him."

"With the handy stake you happen to have in your—pocket?"

She glared at him. She was dressed, once again, in his gym shorts and a T-shirt, one so old it was no longer black, but gray. Barefoot. He was slightly more respectable looking in faded jeans, loafers, and an orange T-shirt the color of a traffic cone. "It's a restaurant," she said, faking a confidence she didn't feel. "We'll find a big sharp knife and cut his lying head off with it."

Burke shrugged.

"You really don't have a problem with this?"

"He killed you and your friend and who knows how many other girls. I'll eat his heart and have room for a big breakfast."

She opened her mouth, and promptly closed it. Other girls? Horrifying thought! Of course Pete hadn't stopped with Maggie. And it had been years. *Decades.* How many—

"And he doesn't have to kill them," she said out loud, bitterness like acid on her tongue. "You don't have to kill them. People give more blood to the Red Cross."

"Yes, Serena."

"He didn't have to! I would have—I would have forgiven him for what he did to me, but he didn't have to kill Maggie, too." She sobbed dryly into her hands, amazed that after all this time, she could still cry for Maggie. For herself. She felt Burke's hand on her shoulder, firm, as he pulled her across the seat and into his side.

"You're right, Serena. The beast doesn't have to kill to feed. You're not an animal like I am."

That thought shocked her—she had never thought of Burke as an animal. Not once. She was the bad one. He was—he was Burke.

She rested her head on his shoulder and watched as his reliable blue Ford ate up the miles.

Chapter 12

"Party town," she commented, staring at the throngs of people, the dozens of cars crammed taillight to headlight all along the streets.

"Yes," Burke said, illegally parking the truck. "It'll be like this until Labor Day."

"Provincetown. P-town?"

"There you go. You sound like a local."

"I'm not moving out here after—after. I can't stand the accent."

"Yah, sure, you betcha," he teased. "Because you don't have an annoying twangy Minnesota accent. You sound like an extra from *Fargo.*"

"Shut up. I hate that movie. And can we focus, please?" She opened the door and hopped out of the truck, but he was already out and coming around the front. He took her

hand in a firm grip and led her to the front door of Eat
Me Raw.

"Wait! Shouldn't we . . . uh . . . be subtle?"

"We're here to kill the beast," he said. "It's best to get it
done."

"So we'll just go in there and ask for him?"

"That was the plan, right?"

"What if he's not here?"

"If he's like most restaurant owners, he's here seven days a
week, two-thirds of every day. Night, I mean. Good place to
troll for victims. And here?" He gestured to the teeming
crowds, the bars, the bright lights, the chaos. On a Tuesday
night, no less. "Who would notice a vampire here? Or a missing girl right away?"

"Nobody missed me," she admitted. "I didn't have any
family, and nobody believed Maggie. The cops assumed I'd
hit the road. Maggie wouldn't let it go and they finally listed
me as a Missing Person."

He scowled. "That sucks. I would have knocked over
houses to find you. Strung men up by their balls."

Touched, she said, "That's so sweet, Burke."

He shoved open the door of the restaurant and walked in.
She felt as though they were actually pressing against the
noise from the bar. It was a typical New England raw bar—
bright lights and dark wood and yakking tourists. Burke
shouldered his way past them and walked up to the hostess
stand.

"I'm sorry," the hostess practically screamed, "but there's
a ninety-minute wait!"

"We'd like to see the owner!" Burke bellowed back. His voice climbed effortlessly over the din and several women (and not a few men) turned to look. "Tell him an old friend from Minnesota is here!"

"Scream a little louder, why don't you?" she muttered, knowing his werewolf hearing would pick it up. "I'm sure the cops will never be able to find a witness or ten."

As the hostess yelled into one of those cell phone/walkie-talkie things, he turned to her and replied, "We're here to kill a dead man. Tough case for the cops to solve. His birth certificate, assuming they can I.D. him when we finish, is probably just a bit out of date. Legally, he probably doesn't exist."

"He *shouldn't* exist," she muttered.

"I'm sorry!" the hostess yelled. "He's not in the bar right now!"

"She's lying," he said. "I can smell it."

"Well, let's—"

"It's all right, Annie," a stranger said, materializing beside the hostess. "No need to cover for me this time. I'll be glad to talk to these people."

Serena felt Burke jump, and knew why: no scent. She looked at Pete and was a little surprised. The boogeyman, the monster, the thing that haunted her dreams and stole her rest was a balding man in his early forties. Well. Who looked like he was in his early forties. What little hair he had left was going gray. His eyes were a light mud brown, and his nose was too small for his face. He was neatly dressed in a dark suit the color of his hair. He looked like a nurse shark: harmless, with teeth.

He smiled at her. She was startled to see he knew her at once. "Sorry about your friend."

She tried to speak. Couldn't. And she knew—*knew*—why he was smiling. He thought he was safe. His turf, his town. All these *people*. He thought they wouldn't touch him. And he was *old*. For vampires, age meant strength. He thought if worse came to terrible, he could take them.

"Let's step outside," Burke said, and seized Pete by the arm.

"I don't think so," the old monster said loudly. "I'm needed here. I—hey!" They tussled for a moment, and then Burke literally started dragging him toward the rear of the restaurant. Serena could see shock warring with dignity on Pete's face: make a fuss and get help? Or endure and get rid of them outside?

She could see him try to set his feet, and see his amazement when Burke overpowered him again, almost effortlessly. She could also see the way Burke's jaw was set, the throbbing pulse at his temple. It wasn't just werewolf strength; Burke was overpowering the monster with sheer rage.

"Killing girls," Burke was muttering, as the armpit of Pete's suit tore. He got a better grip. "Killing girls. *Killing girls!*"

A few people stared. But this was P-town and nobody interfered. New Englanders were famous for minding their own business.

"What the hell are you?" Pete yelled back. "You're no vampire!"

"I'm worse," Burke said through gritted teeth. They were in the kitchen now, the smell of sizzling chicken wings making Serena want to gag. "I *have* to kill to eat."

Before any of the staff could react—or even notice, as hard as they were all working—Serena hurried ahead. She figured she might as well contribute to the felony kidnapping in some small way, so she held the back door open for them. Burke dragged Pete out, past the reeking garbage rollaways, past the illegally parked cars, past the boardwalk, onto the beach. Serena bent and picked up a piece of driftwood, one about a foot long and shaped, interestingly, like a spear. She could feel the splinters as she held it in her hand; it was about two inches in diameter.

Pete swung and connected; the blow made Burke stagger but he didn't loosen his grip. "Your pack leader didn't authorize this," he said. "You'll start a war."

Ah, the monster knew about werewolves—that was interesting. Of course, it made sense . . . Pete would want to know who he was sharing the killing field with.

"Serena's my pack. And you're all rogues. Don't pretend you're Europe. Nobody will miss you."

"Nobody missed you," Pete leered at her.

"Not then. But now, yes." She hefted the driftwood, then hesitated, hating herself for it but unable to resist. "Why? Why me, and why Maggie?"

"And Cathie and Jenny and Barbie and Kirsten and Connie and Carrie and Yvonne and Renee and Lynn and so many I've lost count. Why? Are you seriously asking me that? Why? Because that's what we do, stupid. You're—what? Fifty-some years old and you don't know that?"

"We don't do that," she retorted, and gave him a roundhouse smack of her own. "We don't *do* that! We don't have to!

You did it because you *wanted* to!" Each shout was punctuated with another blow; Burke and Pete were skidding and sliding in the sand. The sea washed over their ankles. She had to scream to be heard over the surf. That was all right. She felt like screaming. She was, literally, in a killing rage. "You wanted to! She never did *anything* bad and you wanted to!"

"It's what we do," Pete said again, black blood trickling from his mouth, his nose. "The king won't stand for this."

"Who do you think *sent* me, bastard? He's getting rid of every one of you tinpot tinshit dictators. He won't stand for your shit and neither will I!"

"Then why," Pete said, and spat out two teeth, "why are you still talking?"

Good question. She kicked him in the balls while she thought of an answer. She had the stake. She had the anger. She even had a henchman. So why was the monster still alive?

"We don't do that," she said at last, and dropped the stake. She was condemning who knew how many more women to torture and death . . . Maggie was counting on her, wherever she was, and—and— "We don't do that and I don't do that."

"Ha," Pete said, and grinned at her through broken teeth. "All the way from Minnesota. Long trip for nothing."

"Not nothing," Burke said. "She came for me. She just didn't know." Then he broke Pete's neck, a dry snap swallowed by the waves. Pete's mouth was opening and closing like a goldfish in a bowl, and then—Serena couldn't believe it—and then Burke literally ripped the monster's head off and tossed it away like a beach ball. The sound it made was like a chicken leg being pulled from a thigh. Times a thousand.

She spun away from their little group of evil and tried to be sick in the sand, but couldn't vomit. The sound—and the look on Pete's face when his neck broke—and the *sound*—

Burke briskly washed his hands in the surf and knelt beside her. She leaned against him and wiped her mouth.

"I knew you wouldn't," he whispered into her ear. "I told you: I'm the beast, not you."

"I just—couldn't. He was smirking at me and he knew I couldn't and he just—I just—" She closed her eyes and heard the snap of Pete's neck breaking again. This time it didn't make her feel sick. This time it made her . . . not exactly happy. More like . . . peaceful? "Oh, Burke. What if you hadn't come? What if I'd never met you?"

"But I did. And you did. And Maggie can rest. No more bad dreams."

"How did you know I—?"

He kissed her on the temple. "How could I not know my own mate?"

She clung to him, ignoring the surf wetting their legs, their knees. "Your mate? You still want to—?"

"Since you were in the hole and told me to go away. I couldn't leave you then. How could I leave you now? You're for me and I'm for you."

"Just like that?"

He shrugged.

"Just like that," she answered herself. The events of the past two days flashed across her mind: all he had done. For her. Had anyone ever . . . ? Who else could have done so much for her, but the man she was destined to be with?

"I'll outlive you," she said tearfully.

"On the upside, I can't knock you up."

"No kids," she said, cheering up.

He kissed her again. "No kids."

They rose as one and walked to the truck, not looking back when the surf covered Pete's body—both pieces—and took it away.

As predicted, nobody missed him, except the liquor rep, and she quickly found a new client.

No one in the bar who saw Burke and Serena ever forgot them, and no one in the bar ever saw them again. Drifters, in and out of P-town, two of several thousand tourists who came through Cape Cod each summer. Nothing special about them.

No, nothing at all.

Witch
Way

To my husband,
who is my opposite in every way:
politically, religiously, economically, and neurologically.
Do I believe in love at first sight? You bet!
Do I believe opposites attract?
I have two children (both look like him)
who would testify to that fact.

ACKNOWLEDGMENTS

Thanks again to Cindy Hwang at Berkley, who never clutches her head (at least in my presence) when I pitch a new idea. And thanks to the fabulous cover artists and the flap copy techs; I could never sum up a book (or four novellas) in two paragraphs, but those bums make it look easy.

AUTHOR'S NOTE

Not all witches were bad. Not all witches were even witches, particularly during the madness of the Salem witch trials.

But some were. And they got pissed. That's all I've got to say about that.

She turned me into a newt! It got better.

—MONTY PYTHON AND THE HOLY GRAIL

My mother says I must not pass
Too near that glass.
She is afraid that I will see
A little witch that looks like me.
With a red mouth to whisper low
The very thing I should not know.

—SARAH MORGAN BRUAMT PIATT,

THE WITCH IN THE GLASS

There is no hate lost between us.

—*THE WITCH*, ACT IV, SC. 3

There is no love lost between us.

—CERVANTES, *DON QUIXOTE*, BOOK IV

Prologue

Tucker Goodman did not take his hat off, a whipping offense if anyone else dared try it. He pointed a long, bony finger at the witch in the blocks and said, in a voice trembling with rage and age, "You are an unnatural thing, cast out by the devil to live among good people—"

"Good people," the witch said, craning (and failing) to look at him, "like the Swansons? You know perfectly well the last three littluns born on that farm weren't got on the missus, but instead, the eldest daughter. Not to mention—"

"Liar!" Farmer Swanson was on his feet, his face purpling, while Mrs. Swanson just huddled deeper into the bench and cried softy into her handkerchief. "That *thing* filled my girls' heads with lies!"

"Silence, Farmer Swanson!" Silence reigned, as the witch knew it would. There was no reasoning with a mob. Unless you were the leader of the mob.

"I think we can all agree—"

"That you're a creaky old man who likes having marital congress with fifteen-year-olds to keep the evil spirits away." The witch laughed.

"—that since you were sent here, there has been naught but wickedness afoot."

"Except for all the children I cured of the waxing disease," the witch pointed out helpfully.

No one said anything. The witch wasn't surprised. Say just the wrong thing at the wrong time, and things like guilt or innocence didn't matter. Defend a witch, and you'd be burned alive, too. Just a handy scapegoat to roast and dance about. That's all they really wanted.

"You will die in agony, yet cleansed by fire."

"Terrific," the witch muttered.

"And in penance for your evil deeds, your children and your children's children, down through the ages, will be persecuted and hunted until you share your powers with your greatest enemy."

"I see no logic in that order of things," the witch commented. "Why not just kill me and get it over with?"

"Because you keep coming back," Goodman said, clearly exasperated. "My great-great-grandfather told me all about you. You bring your mischief to the town and have your fun and then are burned and show up in another town a few years later."

"I like to keep busy."

"This time, if you don't give over your powers to your greatest enemy, you'll be doomed to walk the earth forever, alone and persecuted."

"And if I do give over my powers to my greatest enemy?"

Goodman smirked, revealing teeth blackening with age. "But you never will, unnatural thing. You don't have a heart to share, to open. And so I curse you, as this town curses you, doomed to walk the earth forever, alone."

"How very Christian and forgiving of you," the witch muttered.

Goodman, wrapped tightly in his cloak of smug judgment, ignored the witch's comment. Instead, he sprinkled a foul-smelling herb poultice in the witch's hair and clothes, ignoring the sneezes, then stood back as flaming chunks of wood were tossed, arcing through the air and landing on the pile of wood the witch was standing on.

The witch wriggled, but the town elders knew their business: The witch was trussed as firmly to the center pole as a turkey on a spit. An unpleasant comparison, given what was happening right now . . .

"Well, if I *do* come back," the witch shouted over the crackling flames, "you can bet I will never set foot in Massachusetts again!" Then, as his feet caught fire, Christopher de Mere muttered, "Fie on this. Fie all *over* this."

The villagers watched the man turn into a living candle, making the sign of the cross, as he hardly made a sound, except for the occasional yelp of pain or muttered taunt. And later, scraping through the ashes, they never found a single bone.

Things were quiet.

For a while.

Rhea Goodman sat at the broad wooden table in her mother's farmhouse and waited expectantly. Her parents, Flower and Power (real names: Stephanie and Bob), were looking uneasy, and Rhea felt in her bones that It Was Time.

Time to explain why she'd been brought up a nomad, moving from commune to commune.

Time for Flower and Power to explain why they clung to the hippie thing, even though they were in their fifties and ought to have ulcers and IBM stock.

Time to explain her younger sister's insistence on playing "kill the witch! kill the witch!" with the kid as the hero and her as the witch.

Her theory? Flower and Power had robbed a bank. Or blown up a building. Because they were on the run, no question.

Only . . . from whom?

And her little sister was just weird.

"Rhea, baby, we wanted to sit you down and have a talk." Flower ran her long, bony fingers through her graying red hair, waist length and for once not pulled back in the perpetual braid.

"About your future," Power added, rubbing his bald, sunburned pate. He was about three inches shorter than her mother, who, at five-five, wasn't exactly Giganto. She had passed both of them in height by the time she was fourteen. "And your past."

"Super-duper." She folded her hands and leaned forward. "And whatever you guys did, I'm sure you had to do. So I forgive you."

"It wasn't us," Flower said, sitting down, then changing her mind and standing. Then sitting again. The sun was slanting through the western windows, making the table look like it was on fire, and for the first time in memory, Rhea saw her mother wince away from the light. "It was destiny."

Yeah, you were destined to rob a bank. Or free test animals. And then have kids and spend the rest of your life on the run. Homeschooling, ugh!

"As the eldest—"

"Yeah, where *are* the other ankle biters, anyway?" Rhea had four brothers and sisters: Ramen, Kane, Chrysanthemum, and Violet, aged nineteen, fifteen, twelve, and eight, respectively.

"Away from here. This is business strictly for the eldest of the family. For centuries it has been this way."

Abruptly, Flower started to cry. Power got up and clumsily patted her. "We can't tell her," she sobbed into her work-roughened hands. "We just can't!"

"We must," Power soothed.

"Hey, whoa, it's all right!" She held her hands up in the universal "simmer down" motion. "Whatever you did, it's cool with me." *Good God, did they kill someone?* "I'm sure we can figure something out."

"It's not what we did, it's what you're going to do."

"Go back to college? Forget it. Like the man said, it's high school with ashtrays. Get a new job? Working on it. Try to get one of my poems published? Working on that, too."

"No," Flower said, lips trembling. "Nothing like that."

"Then what is it?"

"It's destiny."

"Yeah, great, what does that mean?"

"You're going to kill the greatest evil to walk the earth, and you'll die in the process," Power told her. "So it is, so it has been, so it shall be. Only if the hunter makes the ultimate sacrifice will the witch be vanquished." He sounded like he was quoting from a book. Then he continued, and his voice no longer sounded like a recitation. "I'm so sorry, Rhea. I'm just so, so sorry."

Her mother was beyond contributing to the conversation and simply cried harder.

Rhea felt her mouth pop open in surprise. "So, uh, you

guys didn't rob a federal bank?" Then, "Don't tell me all those fairy stories you told me about witches and witch-hunters and demons are *true*. Because if they are—"

Flower and Power nodded.

"Jinkies," she muttered and rested her sharp little chin on her folded hands.

Chapter 2

Chris Mere tried. He really did. If his family history wasn't reason enough not to draw attention to himself, ever, the fact that he had parked in a rough neighborhood was.

But the girl was screaming. *Screaming.* And as he approached, he could hear the man ripping her clothes, talking to her in a hissing whisper, could see the moonlight bounce off the blade he held at her neck.

Chris cleared his throat. "Uh. Excuse me?"

Victim and would-be rapist both looked at him.

"Yeah, uh. Could you, uh, not do that?"

"Fuck off, white bread. Me and the bitch got bidness."

"I guess you didn't hear. Times have changed. *No* means *no*, and all that. And it looks to me like the lady is saying *no*. Emphatically. So why don't you let her go, before I turn you into a turnip?" *And what the hell rhymes with turnip, anyway?*

"You come any closer, I cut the bitch!"

"With what?"

"You blind? With this!"

"You who have a knife at her throat

Put it down or be turned into . . . shit!"

They were both staring at him. And the knife was still jammed against the underside of the woman's chin.

"What's this? Rhyming an' shit?"

"Help me, you idiot," the woman practically hissed, glaring at him.

"Wait, wait, I've got it." Chris closed his eyes and concentrated on the mental image he needed.

"If you keep robbing ladies,

You'll come down with rabies.

Not to mention scabies."

"Stop with the poetry and call. The. Police," the woman grated.

"Man, you are *nuts.* You—" He stopped suddenly and clutched his throat. "Oh, man . . . I am so hot. Are you guys hot?" He coughed and spat and spat again. "Where am I? Who the hell are you guys?" He dropped the knife. "I've got to get out of here!"

"That seems like a good plan," Chris agreed.

"I-I—garrggh!" The would-be rapist started foaming at the mouth and actually barked at him.

"What the hell?" the woman said, twisting away from her assailant. "Did you just give him *rabies*?"

"Uh, yeah."

"Will he die?" The woman warily watched Sir Foams-a-Lot, as he darted in and out of a nearby alley.

"No, it's only temporary. Of course, every time he tries to bother a lady, it'll come back. Either that," he added thoughtfully, "or scabies will get him. That's some kind of skin condition, isn't it?"

"He was right," the woman said, backing away from him. "You're nuts."

"Hey!" he yelled at her rapidly departing form. "Don't thank me or anything!"

She waved a hand over her shoulder, but never slowed down.

Chris sighed and kept walking, stepping over the knife like most men would step over dog poop. He was not really thinking about what he was doing, he was just automatically avoiding something unpleasant. He thought about turning it into a banana, but for the life of him couldn't remember anything that rhymed with banana.

Why did he even bother? They never hung around. No matter what he did for them, what magic he could make, they always got scared and ran away. For two cents, he'd give them something to *really*—

He stopped walking and pressed his palms over his eyes. *Don't think like that. You're one of the good guys, remember?*

Yeah, sure. As if he could fight three centuries of ingrained behavior.

You'd better.

Or what?

You know what.

He snorted. His inner voice sounded weirdly like his late grandfather . . . who had been killed by a witch-hunter from the Goodman line. His father had died at the hands of a Goodman twenty years later.

Now it was his turn. Unless he could prove to Goodman that he wasn't a danger to society.

Because if *he* could fight three centuries of conditioning, *she* sure as hell could.

Hell, he was as much of a demon fighter as a witch . . . how many demons had he vanquished? How many lives had he saved?

Did you do it for them, or for you?

What difference did it make?

But sometimes, when sleep wouldn't come, he'd burn with the desire for revenge. The Goodmans had been killing his family for centuries. Wasn't it time the de Meres got back some of their own?

He'd shove the thought away, try to be a good enough guy, but it always came back. Freakin' *always*.

Mixed feelings or not, he'd spent the last five years tracking down just about all the Goodmans in the country. And he had satisfied himself that, in every past case, the surname was just a coincidence. And he'd had many pleasant conversations as a result . . . and even a few free meals. Not that, as a Mere, he needed free anything. But still, they had been nice. They gave him hope for what was to come.

Annoyingly, the last batch lived in—ugh—Massachusetts. Salem, to be exact.

Salem. Just reading the name on a map gave him chills, never mind driving there.

Salem, land of the disenchanted and intolerant. Salem, the killing grounds for twenty accused witches (only one of which, by the way, had been a witch). Salem, where hundreds were accused of witchcraft during the rising hysteria between June and September 1692.

Come to think of it, he probably should have started there and saved himself several years of looking, but he couldn't bring himself to take that step until it was absolutely necessary. As far as he knew, a Mere hadn't set foot in Massachusetts in more than two hundred years, maybe longer. And there was a good reason for that. The freakin' state motto was, "By the Sword We Seek Peace," for God's sake! No, he had been right to avoid the state, at least until it was absolutely necessary to his plan.

Unfortunately, now it was. It gave him the creeps to even be crossing the state line, never mind lurking in Boston's dark alleys, tracking down more friggin' Goodmans and vanquishing the occasional smelly demon.

Not that he expected the witch-hunter to be listed in the Yellow Pages under "Hunters, Witch." Fortunately, lots of things rhymed with Goodman, and his magic was helping him methodically track them all down. And—and maybe it was just a fable, after all. Maybe all his antecedents had died of natural causes.

Ha. Were being burned at the stake or hanged on the gallows natural causes anywhere but Salem?

Still, he'd go. Then he'd talk, try to make peace. If only Goodman wouldn't set him on fire before he could explain that he was one of the good guys . . .

Assuming he actually was. Sometimes he wasn't too sure.

Chapter 3

"Again, Rhea. Again!"

Panting, she lowered the crossbow and glared at her father. "I don't see you out here slinging arrows of misfortune. And for an ex-hippie, you know entirely too much about how to kill people."

"I watched my father train my older brother," Power replied, absently running his hand over his bald spot—a sure sign he was distressed. "We never did find his body."

"Oh, *great*." Disgusted, she aimed the crossbow, and the arrow thwacked the mannequin right in the groin.

"That's not a lethal wound," her father snapped.

"No, but I bet he wishes it was."

"Rhea, stop it! This is a serious business. You have to fulfill your destiny, to—"

"That's another thing. Why did you wait until now to tell me?"

"Think, Rhea. Why?"

She sighed and reloaded the crossbow. "Don't even tell me. Twenty-first-birthday ritual?" Oh, *great*. She'd been legal-drinking-age for twelve whole hours and was doomed to kill a powerful magic user and get killed in the process. "So you let me have twenty-one years of blissful ignorance, is that the way it works?"

Power nodded.

"Great. Any idea when Hot Shit Magic Guy is going to show up?"

"You've got a couple more years to train. So we have to be ready. Again."

None of the weapons were new to her. She'd been training (for fun, she had thought) in the barn for more than ten years. But shooting a man-shaped mannequin or a scarecrow wasn't the same as pointing a gun or a crossbow or a knife at a real man and finding the will to drive home a lethal stroke.

She'd never killed anything in her life. Heck, she'd never even swatted a fly.

But her parents pooh-poohed her worries, telling her that killing was in her blood, that with proper training she would do her duty when the time came.

"For what?" she had asked.

Her mother had finally stopped crying. "What do you mean, Rhea?"

"What's the point? According to you guys, another witch and another Goodman—one of the ankle biters' kids, I'm betting—will be born in the next generation, and the whole stupid thing starts all over again."

"Your point?" her father had asked.

"Why do it at all? It's fruitless."

"We do it," her mother had said, sounding firm for once, "because it is our family duty. And we do it to rid the world of evil. I don't want to lose you, Rhea, but I'll see you dead by my own hand before I'll let you turn your back on the world, on your family."

"Great, Mother. Just wonderful."

Still trying to reconcile the fact that her parents were fine with seeing her dead—by a witch or by their hands—Rhea groped for her Beretta and obliterated the mannequin's face with eight rounds.

It didn't make her feel much better.

Chapter 4

Chris drove the rental car through the gate and up the winding driveway, admiring the trees lining the drive, their leaves in full summer glory. *It must be amazing in the fall*, he thought.

The house and barn loomed before him, the barn a traditional red, the two-story house cream-colored with black shutters. Horses grazed in the field beside the barn, their coats glossy in the July sun. It was too idyllic for a hotbed of born-and-bred killers, which cheered him. He braked, yanked on the parking break, shut off the engine, and got out.

Just in time to practically shit his pants when a voice behind him shrilled, "Kill the witch! Kill the witch!"

He whirled, frantically trying to think of a rhyme to save himself, only to see a girl around seven years old pointing a toy six-shooter at him.

"Yeesh," he said.

"Kill the witch! Pschow, pschow!" She aimed the toy gun between his eyes and fired twice. She was grinning hugely, showing the gap between her front teeth, the sun bouncing off the golden highlights in her light brown hair, dark eyes sparkling with fun. "You're dead, witch!"

"Uh, run along, kiddo."

"You're dead, witch!"

"Okay. Bye now."

With a final "pschow!" she darted past him and up the porch steps, disappearing around the corner.

Chris took long, steadying breaths. *Okay. I clearly have not prepared for this encounter. It's okay. Deep breath. The kid caught you off guard, and you're on edge anyway, because nobody's tried the "let's just talk" approach, ever. And you're breaking years of tradition by showing up before your official "coming of age" ceremony. Deep breaths.*

He attached little importance to the witch game; the kid had, after all, grown up in Salem. They probably soaked up "kill the witch" with their mother's milk. Instead, he shrugged off the encounter and mounted the front porch steps, then rapped politely at the front door.

It was opened almost immediately by a middle-aged woman, late forties or early fifties, a woman who would have looked very nice if her eyes weren't so red and swollen. *Allergies*, he thought. *Or she's been crying for a while.*

"Yes?" she asked in a watery voice.

"Uh, hello, I'm looking for your eldest."

"My—you mean Rhea?" She pulled a tissue out of her sleeve and blew her nose. "Who are you? Are you from her school?"

"My name's Chris Mere," he replied, not expecting much in the way of consequences. He'd done this thousands of times in the past five years.

So the woman's reaction was startling, to say the least. Her eyes widened, then narrowed, and she started to slam the door, on his foot, which he'd thrust forward.

Bingo!

"You get out of here, foul thing! You're two years too early!"

"I like to plan ahead. Uh, ma'am, you're crushing my foot."

"Pity it isn't your head," she snarled, shoving harder.

"Look, I just want to—ow—talk. I'm not here for a fight."

"Too bad," the woman replied, half a second before a walloping pain slammed into his left ass cheek.

He staggered and went down on one knee. "Ow, damn it!"

"You get away from her *right now*," a female voice said coldly, behind him and to his left.

Shot me in the back, he thought, astonished. He clutched his ass and fell on his side. His other side, luckily. *One of the friggin' Goodmans* shot *me in the back!* The pain of it was like nothing in the world; the thing felt like it was coming out his belly button.

He heard steps running up the porch and rolled his eye up to see her. Arrows? Flying? Flying arrows? No, arrows flying true. That was it, by God.

"Rhea, watch out! You're not ready yet!"

Rhea, he thought.

She pointed the crossbow at his forehead. Not ready, his bleeding butt! He assumed she was the eldest Goodman; she looked about the right age. And the good looks he'd hardly noticed in the child and hadn't seen in the mother were unmistakable in this one.

She stared down at him, and time seemed to slow down, giving him a chance to take in her excellent good looks. Shoulder-length brown hair with gold and red highlights. Fair skin, freckled nose. Big dark eyes, currently narrowed to thoughtful slits. About five-seven, one-thirty. A foxy little pointed chin. Curves in all the right places, though the muscle definition was clear, because she was wearing khaki shorts and a red tank top. Red, the color of blood.

Her finger tightened on the trigger. From his vantage point (writhing in pain on the front porch) the arrow looked very, very big and very, very sharp. He could actually see her finger whitening as she slowly squeezed. Summer sunlight bounced off the arrow's silver tip.

I'm going to be killed, he thought, *by the prettiest girl I've ever seen.*

Chapter 5

Rhea heard the car come up the drive, but paid little attention. Her parents were always having friends over, salesmen often called (her parents were notorious for having trouble saying "no, thanks"), old school chums dropped by, people occasionally got lost in the country and stopped for directions. So she kept practicing until her father decided to check the stock. Then she made her escape.

Fuck destiny, she thought. *It's too nice a day to think about killing. Or being killed.*

Weapons were so much a part of her upbringing that she actually forgot to put the crossbow and quiver away; the bow was like an extension of her hand, and she didn't even notice the weight of the quiver. By the time she realized it, she saw her mother try to slam the door on the tall stranger.

In all Rhea's twenty-one years, her mother had *never* slammed the door. Not even on the Jehovah's Witnesses.

So she shot him. Not to kill. To get him to remove his foot from the bottom of the doorway. And it worked splendidly. He went down like a ton of saltwater taffy. She was more than a little amazed; had she worried so much, just an hour ago, about her ability to wound or kill?

She darted up the steps in time to see the tall man curl on his side like a shrimp and frown up at her.

"Rhea, watch out!" her mother shrilled. "You're not ready yet!"

She stared down at him, bringing the crossbow up in slow motion. At least, that's what it felt like. Everything was happening so slowly, she had plenty of time to get a good look at the guy.

Unmistakable: a de Mere. Short, sandy blond hair. Eyes the color of wet leaves. Tall, very tall (his head had almost touched the top of the doorway, before she shot him). Thin, but his broad shoulders were in evidence through his black T-shirt. His long legs looked even longer in the tight, faded jeans.

He looked exactly like the pictures of the de Mere her great-great-great-great- (how many greats was that?) grandfather had burned at the stake (except for the modern clothing). She had seen the archives, the drawings. *Fairy stories*, she had thought. About witches and the warriors who protected the world from their evil. And the demons some of the witches would call forth.

At last, the crossbow was in place. Her finger tightened on the trigger. *This is it! I'm going to kill him on my own front porch, and I'll live to a ripe old age. Why the hell were my folks so scared of him?*

"*Arrows, arrows, flying true,*" he rasped.

"*Form instead a cloud of blue.*"

The arrow in his butt vanished in a puff of blue smoke. The arrow loaded in her crossbow vanished as well. And her quiver suddenly felt pretty light. Horribly light.

"That's better," he mumbled, climbing to his feet with difficulty. He staggered for a few seconds, clutched his butt, then muttered,

"*Arrow's wound paining me,*

Form instead a—shit!"

"Are those supposed to be poems?" Rhea asked, reaching for her Beretta, then remembering she'd locked it in the barn after practice. *Oh, great.*

"You shot me in the back," he snapped, still massaging his ass. His hands were red to the wrist. "That's why I'm the good guy, and you're the bad guys."

"The hell!" she almost shouted, then realized her mother was still standing in the doorway, utterly shocked. Rhea darted forward, shoved her mom back, and slammed the door. Meanwhile, the witch was hobbling around the porch, dripping blood all over the place and mumbling "Ooh, ow, ouch, God help me, ow ow ow . . ."

"You're wrong," she snapped, freshly outraged. How dare he accuse her of villainy? He'd come to her home uninvited and terrorized her mother. For that last one, if nothing else, she'd see him dead.

Her blood was still humming; her heartbeat thundered in her ears. She itched for a weapon, or a stake, some rope, and a box of fireplace matches. Because she wanted to kill him. She needed to kill him. Everything that was in her, centuries of tradition, cried out for it.

It was like, until she saw him in the flesh, her life had been rudderless.

"The hell," he retorted, and she tried to remember what they had been talking about. "I've never shot anybody in the back in the twenty-eight years *I've* been running around on the planet. You can't say the same, Rhea. Hell, your little sister runs around yelling 'kill the witch' at complete strangers."

"Shut up." She wondered if she could kick him to death. Surely it was worth a try. "You're the foul evil magicks bringer and demon raiser, not me. *I'm* protecting the world from *you*. It's not the other way around."

"Magic," he sighed, straightening. "And I don't *raise* them. I just get rid of them. That's an old wives' tale, that we raise demons. *Magicks*. Jesus!"

"What?"

"Not magicks. Magic. I can hear the '*ck*,' and you're wrong about that, too. What rhymes with wound?"

"Boon, dune, croon, cartoon, commune, swoon . . ." she answered automatically. She'd been studying poetry since the seventh grade. Her other talent, you might say.

"Swoon!" he shouted. "That's it.

Unkind arrow, leaving a wound,
Fix me up before I swoon."

She gasped as the bleeding stopped, as the blood disappeared from his hands, as he straightened up with a sigh. "Oh, God, that's so much better. Christ, my aching ass."

Okayyyy. So, her parents were right to be scared shitless by this guy. It seemed her ancestors had the right idea: Wipe out the de Mere line, witch by witch. Funny, in all the archives and all the old records and during her training, no one had mentioned he could *bend the very fabric of reality to his will*.

"Nobody told me you could bend the very fabric of reality to your will."

"Gee, so sorry your intel isn't up to snuff. No pun intended."

"I thought you were supposed to curse cows and sour their milk, or be a bride of Satan, or something like that."

He stared at her, green eyes wide. "Do I look like I spend my days hanging around cows? And I'm not a bride of anything."

"Why didn't the archives mention your little poetry trick?" she mused aloud, not really expecting an answer.

"Nobody knows, except you Goodmans. My great-great-great-great-grandfather couldn't."

"Not enough greats."

"Never mind. Anyway, Christopher de Mere couldn't do it, and none of his descendants could, for the longest time. And FYI, we dropped the 'de' about four generations ago."

"What do you mean, they couldn't do it? You can all do magic."

He nodded and even smiled. She couldn't believe they were having a civilized conversation.

She still wanted to kill him, though.

"Oh, they could do magic," he replied, "but it was a lot harder—I mean, would real witches allow themselves to be burned at the stake if they could save themselves? Oh, and that's quite a family history of murder, mayhem, and close-mindedness you've got there."

"Shut *up*. It wasn't just my family," she added lamely. The insanity of the Salem witch trials, deemed so necessary three hundred years ago, were an embarrassment to the Goodmans these days. So many innocents. Not enough of the guilty. "Why are we having a conversation? You're a dead man walking."

"Takes one to know one, sunshine. Except for the 'man' part, of course. And to finish answering your rude and intrusive questions, the Mere family has been evolving each generation in order to better deal with *you* bums. Thus, I rhyme, things happen. I rhyme, your pretty shiny things go bye-bye."

"Oh, *great*."

"I thought so," he admitted.

She abruptly turned and marched down the porch steps, annoyed to hear him following her. "Hey! We're talking, here."

"We're done talking."

"Where are you going?"

"Shut up."

"Are you going into the barn?"

"Shut up."

"Rhea, Rhea, tell me true

What is in the barn for you?"

She felt an invisible hand seize her mouth and force it open. She stopped in her tracks, appalled, and fought with as much inner strength as she could muster, but still her traitorous mouth fell open, and she said, almost babbled, "Four nines, two crossbows, a twelve-gauge shotgun, a twenty-gauge shotgun, ammo for everything, four skinning knives, two filet knives, six switchblades, and a Magnum .357."

"But we were just talking!" he yelled after her, sounding panicked. "There's no need to take out four nines! What the hell is a four nine?"

Since he hadn't done magic, she was not compelled to answer and did not bother to explain that she had four nine-millimeter Berettas in the locked chest under the floor of the barn.

"Don't you want to just talk?" The rhyming moron was still trotting after her. "We don't have to kill each other, you know."

What bullshit! She didn't trouble herself to come up with the scathing remarks he had coming. Instead, she made it to the barn without interference (magical or otherwise), and pulled on the trapdoor on the south side of the building. She leaned down, spun the combination on the safe, popped it open, reached inside, and pulled out two Berettas.

"Rhea, Rhea, with your guns,

Stop this madness before it . . . shit!"

He's not a god, she thought with not a little relief. *He can't rhyme for shit. And thank goodness. Because otherwise, we'd all be cooked.*

She cocked the guns (they were always loaded; no need to even check) and held them up, just in time to see him sprint in the other direction.

Yeah, you'd better run, de Mere.

She started to take the shot

(I've never shot anybody in the back.)

and hesitated. Was it true? Was it cowardly and sneaking and bad-guy-like to take a witch from behind? All her teachings cried out in the negative. But de Mere had the weight of a bunch of Westerns on his side.

Because the bad guys always snuck up and shot you in the back.

These outrageous new thoughts crowded her brain and she hesitated. Not for long, but it gave de Mere time to dive through the driver's-side window. She put plenty of bullets through said window, but either he had perfected the art of driving while kneeling on the mat, or he had made a rhyme that made bullets bounce off, because the next thing she knew, the only thing left of Chris de Mere was a spume of dust in her driveway.

She lowered her now-empty guns and stared at the dust. She'd had the shot, and she bungled it. The Goodmans might be out of luck if they were counting on her to save them.

Chapter 6

A week later, he returned. This time he had scribbled down several words on pink Post-Its, words that rhymed with arrow and Beretta and gun and Rhea. He had been careful to return the bullet-ridden rental and drive up in a different car (the Avis people had not been pleased, to say the least), hoping they wouldn't nuke him the moment he pulled into their driveway.

He convinced himself he was here because it was worth another try, that people could overcome centuries of conditioning, these were modern times, and witch-hunting was just silly.

But the reality was, he couldn't get the trigger-happy jerk out of his head. *That's* why he'd come back. Her "oh, *greats*" and "shut ups" were actually kind of funny. And that hot little figure she had wasn't bad, either. And he loved the pointy little chin. At six-four, he was taller, but he didn't tower over Rhea the way he did with most women.

Worst of all: He couldn't imagine killing her. He'd liked her right away (insanity!), even if she had shot him in the ass. Or maybe *because* she shot him in the ass. She had sure charged up the steps in defense of her mother without hesitation, and he liked that, too.

His parents were long dead. He tried not to blame the Goodmans . . . the one who had done the deed was, after all, also dead. For every Mere death, a Goodman had died, too. He tried to keep it in mind at all times. It helped when he was tempted to abandon the human race, let the demons swarm, and use his magic to win the lottery. Repeatedly.

Anyway, he liked—what was the word? He liked her *moxie*. And frankly, verbally sparring with a woman who could kill him (who was *fated* to kill him) was an unbelievable rush.

He carefully drove up to the house, eyes peeled for Goodmans. But the house and barn looked quiet, and he could see no cars in the drive.

He put the car in park, deliberately left the parking brake alone (it had almost been the death of him last time; he'd wasted valuable seconds releasing it before making his escape), and climbed out.

"Uh . . . hello? Anybody home? Goodmans? Rhea?"

He moved closer to the front porch, then heard a sound to his left and turned in the direction of the barn. "Mr. and Mrs. Goodman? Rhea? Anybody up for a rematch?"

The attack came without warning; he hadn't heard a thing.

But a sturdy weight smacked him in the middle of the back, and he went facedown onto the gravel driveway.

"Kill the witch!" a familiar voice shouted. "Pschow, pschow!"

"Kid," he said into the driveway, "get off me. Seriously."

"Die, evil fiend, die!"

"Kid."

"Pschow!"

"Kid. I'm serious." He tried to move, to gently shift her off his back, but she clung like a lamprey. "I know it's not cool to smack children, especially not your own, but if you don't get off me—"

"Kill the witch!"

"What are they *feeding* you guys? You're, what? Seven? And you're already obsessed with witch-hunting? Jesus wept."

"I'm eight, not seven, stupidhead."

"Thank God. I can't for the life of me think of what rhymes with seven.

Great, great,
Hate, hate,
Off my back
Child of eight."

It was one of his worst rhymes ever (he felt like jumping rope to it), but it had the desired effect; he felt the weight disappear from his back and climbed to his feet. He dusted off his clothes and looked around for the kid.

She was scowling at him from the other side of the rental car. "No fair. You cheater."

"You're one to talk—er, what's your name?"

"Violet Goodman."

"Of course. Anyway, who ambushed who? You Good-mans. Bloodthirsty savages."

"You wait 'til Rhea finds out what you—"

"DID YOU JUST USE MAGIC ON MY BABY SISTER?"

"Uh-oh," Violet said, looking, to her credit, worried for him. Then she added in a much lower voice, "I wasn't really going to tell. You're a good witch, I know."

"Thanks for that." He turned in time to see Rhea come storming down the front steps, headed for him like a flame toward kindling. "Listen, Rhea, Violet jumped me. All I did was pull into your driveway."

"You used *magic* on my *sister.*"

"I didn't hurt her. And before you go running into the arsenal-slash-barn, I warn you that I'm armed with tons of gun-and-arrow rhymes." He patted his pockets, fairly bulging with Post-Its, for emphasis.

She wasn't heading for the barn. She was steaming straight for him, pale face flushed to the eyebrows with rage. He wasn't sure if he was aroused or scared. Or both.

"So don't do anything crazy," he added, standing his ground. "I come in peace, like a benevolent alien. I mean you no harm—ow!"

She'd dropped into a crouch at the last second and swept his legs out from under him with a lunge. Then she was on him, her small hands grasping his neck, squeezing.

"I don't know—if you know—but I can't breathe—when you do that," he gurgled.

"If you can talk," she said grimly, tightening her grip, "you can breathe. How dare you? How dare you come back to my home, threaten my baby sister?" She started to slam his head up and down. Gravel bounced and flew around his ears.

"He didn't threaten me," Violet quickly spoke up. "We were playing."

"Violet. Go in the house."

"But Mom and Dad said you had to play with me when you were watching me, and all you've done is work out in the—"

"Violet. House."

"I don't think you need to choke him," the girl retorted, then reluctantly left.

"I agree," he gasped. The only thing that was saving him was his upper body strength; he had two hands clamped around her wrists, barely holding her off. She might work out like a fiend, but her hands were small, and she couldn't get them all the way around his neck. And it wouldn't be long before she figured that out and starting beating the living shit out of him in earnest. "You should listen to Violet, a kindhearted but slightly disturbed third-grader."

"Don't talk about my sister," she said through gritted teeth, her face going even redder from her strangulation efforts.

Throttle? Bottle? Strangle? What rhymed with strangle? Maybe he could turn her hands into flippers. Flipper, slipper?

Oh, to hell with it. He tightened his grip on her wrists and abruptly rolled over. *Thank you, Mother Nature, for making me a guy.*

Now he was on top, still encircling her wrists with his

fingers, and she glared up at him with such malevolence that he almost let go of her. Which would have been a disaster.

"Okay," he said, and coughed, politely turning his face away. He hated to think how his throat would feel if she'd had bigger hands. "Okay. Listen. I just came here to—"

"Get the *hell* off me!"

"—talk and try to convince you that this is a dance we don't have to do—"

"I am going to kill you a *lot*."

"—because after all, this is the twenty-first century, and don't you think witch-hunting should have been left behind with slavery?"

"Not as long as any de Mere descendants are running around on the planet. Now *let go*!"

"Oh, shut up," he said, and bent down and kissed her.

She went rigid with astonishment, which was a relief, because he didn't care to be bitten at the moment. He'd just meant to give her a peck, but the taste of her soft, sweet mouth worked on him like a hormone shot, and he slid his tongue between her lips, tasting her, relishing her the way he relished a ripe piece of fruit in the summertime.

She didn't make a sound. Just lay there like a board. An amazed, totally shocked board. So he let go of her wrists and cupped her face and deepened the kiss, and he thought he felt her respond, and then—

—and then her face shot out of his line of sight, and he realized she'd slapped him so hard he'd flown off her.

"Ow," he groaned, once again facedown in the dust.

"What did you think you were doing?" He rolled over in

time to see her spring to her feet. "What the hell is wrong with you?"

"Well, at the moment, I've got dust all over me and a piece of gravel up my nose and maybe a nosebleed, too."

She stood over him, jabbing her finger in the air for emphasis. He tried not to flinch. "We are supposed to be killing each other, not kissing. So cool your gonads and get your head in the game."

"That's what I've been trying to tell you," he said patiently, staring up at her. "I'm not in the game. I'm not going to play. I think our families have been killing each other long enough, don't you?"

"As long as a de Mere is around, a Goodman has to kill him."

"Who says?"

Her mouth popped open, and she appeared to be struggling for words, then burst out with, "Everybody! My parents and tradition and—everybody. All the way back to the first Goodman and the first de Mere."

"Yawn," he said.

"It's my duty to kill you and be killed doing it. Just like it's your family duty to try to kill me and be killed doing it."

"Don't you think that's just about the dumbest fucking thing in the world?"

"Well. Yes," she admitted. "But who are we to break from tradition?"

"And that's the second-dumbest thing. Oooof!" She had dropped to her knees—right on his chest. "Gkkk! Air!"

"You listen to me, de Mere. You—"

"Chris," he groaned. "Christopher Mere, do I have to carve it into my forehead?"

"Shut up. You go away and do whatever you have to do until your thirtieth birthday, and I'll do what I have to do, and then the next generation can worry about it."

"Forget it," he gurgled.

"And no more of this showing up at my house being all chatty and shit. Stay away from my family and stay away from me. For the next couple of years at least."

"Sorry. Can't do it."

"You'd *better* do it. And keep your Mere lips to yourself."

"What's wrong with my lips?" He put his hands around her small waist and tossed her off him. She hit the dirt (literally), planted her arms, and spun right back over him.

He shoved. She shoved. Soon they were rolling around in the driveway like a couple of kids having a playground spat.

"Go away!"

"No."

"Buzz off!"

"No."

"I hate you!"

"Well, I hate you, too, sunshine. But you taste pretty good, I must—ow!"

"And don't even *think* about using your rhymes on me. You're a lousy poet and an evil magic-doer."

"Yeah? Well, you come from a long line of cold-blooded murderers."

"I do not!"

"Do, too."

"Not!"

"You totally, completely do."

"Shut up!"

"Make me, sunshine."

"I'll make you, all right." She had temporarily gained the upper hand and was again on top. "I'll make you wish you were never *born*."

"Don't you think we're a little too old for this kind of thing?" He brought his legs up, hooked them around her neck, and rode her all the way down. "Now will you stop trying to beat the hell out of me—ow—and listen? Ouch!" He wondered dizzily if that last punch had given him a concussion.

Beneath him, she wriggled and squirmed in the dirt like an outraged snake. That was actually a big, big problem, because the fight (and the kiss) had seriously turned him on. He prayed she couldn't feel his erection. She'd cut if off. He pressed down harder, careful not to hurt her, inwardly groaning as he tried to hide the biggest boner of his life.

A boner for the witch-hunter! Jesus wept.

"Will you stop wiggling and listen?"

Gasping from her efforts, Rhea wheezed, "There's nothing to listen to."

"Oh, that's the spirit."

"We don't talk, we fight. And kill. You'd better reread your archives."

"Rhea, I can see how it is with you, but you don't know how it is with me. I won't kill you."

She blinked up at him. Her eyes were watering from all

the dust in the air. "You'd better," she said. "Because I'm going to do my damnedest to kill you."

"I won't fight back, Rhea. It'll be murder. Cold-blooded murder."

"It isn't murder."

"It really, really is."

"De Mere, you'd better fight!"

"No."

Before she could screech at him some more, he heard a car pull into the drive, then skid to a halt with the left front tire no more than six inches from the top of Rhea's face.

Car doors were flung open, and quite a few Goodmans piled out and swarmed (how many *were* there, anyway?) around him. He realized he was pinning their eldest into the dirt and the two of them were filthy and sweaty. And their clothes were ripped.

He craned his neck to look up at Rhea's father, who looked about ready to start breathing fire. "Hi, Goodmans. Uh. This isn't what it looks like."

Then somebody came up behind him and turned off all the lights inside his skull.

Chapter 7

Rhea's lips were still burning from the kiss.

She thought of a line from *King of the Hill*: "That boy's not right." It perfectly explained Chris Mere, the big grabby rhyming kissing dolt.

And the bastard was strong. Well, he was big, so she should have expected it, but she'd had no idea how much physical power was lurking within those ropy muscles. She'd tried her very best to beat the hell out of him, and he'd come away from it with only scratches.

But he'd be sore tomorrow, by God.

Her parents had been utterly at a loss. It was inconceivable that a Mere showed up years early, that a Mere was talking peace. Neither of them knew what to do, and both of them thought it might be a trick or a trap of some kind. The de Meres had a centuries-old rep for treachery.

Interestingly, Violet spoke up for him. And Rhea had been forced to admit to Power and Flower that not only had he not hurt the little girl, he'd taken several blows to avoid hurting *her*. That made her folks reel all over again.

After some discussion, they decided it would be disrespectful (not to mention leaving them open to embarrassing questions if someone stopped by) to leave an unconscious Mere in their driveway, so they dragged him inside, all the way to the guest room.

Her mother had hesitantly brought a warm, wet washcloth, tiptoed to the bed, then handed the washcloth to Rhea and hurriedly left, clearly not interested in hanging around the unconscious witch.

Rhea considered gagging him with the washcloth, then gave it up and gently wiped the gravel and small trickles of dried blood off the left side of his face. Once she had that clean enough, she moved to the right side—

—and quick as thought, he was awake and grabbing her wrist, yanking it back from his face. That startled her even more than the kiss, the way he went from flat-out cold unconsciousness to being wide awake, if a little disoriented.

"Oh. It's you. Hey, sunshi—oh, God, my head. My aching, breaking head. How long have I been out?"

"An hour," she said, handing him the washcloth. He folded it into a small square and rested it on his forehead. "Give or take a few minutes."

"Who hit me from behind?" he asked groggily. "Fucking Goodmans; do you ever try a frontal assault?"

"Me," she replied, ignoring the very uncomfortable feeling his comment planted. "I brought my leg up and kicked you in the back of the skull."

"So that's why the room is spinning. I thought we were on a merry-go-round with a bed."

"Not hardly."

"I am totally astonished—yet grateful—to find myself not dead. I don't know how you were all able to restrain yourselves."

"Even we cold-blooded murderers wouldn't slit the vocal cords on an unconscious witch."

"Slit the—"

"Sure. That's how I'll have to kill you. You won't be able to rhyme—make magic—and you'll bleed out in about a minute and a half."

He touched various cuts and scrapes, wincing as he did so. "If anybody can do it, you can."

"Oh, stop."

"No, really."

"You're just saying that."

"No, I'm not. You could absolutely do it."

"Well, thanks. I appreciate that. But if you're feeling better—"

"I am not."

"—you'd better hit the road. My dad's pretty upset, and my mom's not too happy, either."

"Why am I in a bedroom?"

"Well. We couldn't just leave you in the driveway like a dead earthworm."

"How charitable."

"Damn straight, considering the fact that your father killed my dad's older brother."

"I'm pretty sure it was the other way around."

"Either way, time to go."

"But I have contusions," he moaned, as she pulled him into a sitting position. "And possibly a fractured skull. You can't just turn me out into the cold."

"It's eighty degrees outside. And make a rhyme to fix your hurts."

"What rhymes with pain?"

"What doesn't? Chain, brain, drain, mane, main, champagne, bloodstain, complain, disdain, explain, ingrain, migraine—"

"That's it!" he shouted, startling her.
"The man on the bed
With a migraine
Fix his head
And take away his pain."

Rhea covered her eyes. She probably should have covered her ears. "That's really horrible. You're an awful poet."

"Hey, it got the job done, didn't it, sunshine?"

"Quit calling me that."

"Why?"

"We're fated to kill each other, not give each other nicknames like Sunshine and Stupidhead."

He sprang out of the bed, fully healed, and examined his filthy, shredded clothes in the mirror. "I am absolutely billing you for the clothes I must now go buy at Neiman's."

"You will not. And did you hear what I said?"

"Sure. How come you can always come up with a bunch of words that rhyme?"

She studied the pattern of the quilt, rather than look directly at him. She'd been feeling weird, staring at his broad shoulders. Almost . . . tingly? "It was my minor in college. I still, you know, write them. Poems." She wouldn't say it. No, she wouldn't. Okay, maybe she would. "You should get yourself a rhyming dictionary." *Good work! You've just put a powerful weapon into the hands of your greatest enemy.*

"Yeah, well, I don't have a lot of leisure time to hang out in bookstores and—" He spun around so quickly she nearly jumped out the window. "What? You're a poet?"

"Apparently, I'm a warrior for the honor of the Goodman clan," she said dryly.

"Yeah, tell me about it. I got the whole song and dance by the time I was sixteen. How long have you known?"

"Since last Monday," she admitted.

"Oh, shit! Why did your folks wait so long?"

"Tradition."

He had turned back and now scowled at his reflection. "I'm really beginning to hate that word." Then, quick as thought, he spun back. "Wait just one minute. You were going to be a poet, weren't you? But then you had to do . . ." He gestured to his (broad) chest. "This."

"Well . . ." She looked away.

"And you've only known this since *last week*?" He marched to the door and yanked it open. "Where's your dad?"

"Uh . . . target practice, I think."

"Because I'm off to kick his ass."

"Better not," she said, hiding a grin. It wasn't a laughing matter, not really. "He taught me everything I know, not everything he knows."

"I can take him," Chris said confidently.

She snatched up the water glass from the bedside table and flung it toward him, missing his nose (on purpose) by half an inch. The glass exploded against the wall, and he ducked (about two seconds too late).

"What the *hell*?"

"I could have thrown that at your left eye. But I didn't. It's why we always vanquish you, Mere. You can't do magic fast enough to save yourself from our reflexes. All you can do is—"

"Yes?"

"Get your licks in."

"Very nice. I'm out of here. You think I've got nothing better to do than hang out with a girl who wants to ice me?"

"Woman," she corrected.

"Please. I've got almost a decade on you."

"Are you leaving, or do I have to talk to you some more?"

"I am leaving. Right now. I'm sure there's a demon to vanquish or a damsel in distress to rescue."

"Demon?"

"What do you think I do," he snapped, "when I'm not here trying to talk you out of murdering me?"

"Make evil happen?" she guessed.

He rolled his eyes and stomped out the door. She couldn't

help it; she ran to the window and watched as he stormed out, kicking up tufts of dust, then climbed into his car and roared out of the driveway—backward.

"And don't come back!" she shouted after him, wondering why that sounded unconvincing.

Chapter 8

"Where is he?" Power demanded.

"You let him get away?" Flower asked, aghast.

Rhea rubbed her eyes. She *had* let him go. What was wrong with her? Other than being attracted to the man she was supposed to kill. A man who had been very, very careful not to hurt her, despite almost constant provocation. A man she almost wanted to . . . help? Had she gone crazy in the past week? Or had she always been crazy?

Still and all, he sure didn't *seem* evil.

"Answer me," Power said.

"What, you wanted him to spend the night? Have a slumber party with cookies and warm milk? I thought you'd be glad he beat feet out of here, not bummed because you don't have a jammy buddy."

"Watch your mouth."

"The *hell*. You two are egging me on to kill this guy and get killed myself. Then he shows up and not only doesn't kill me, doesn't hurt any one of us. Then he came *back*. And didn't hurt us again."

"He isn't in his prime quite yet. When he has thirty years, he will be formidable. And you. You're already distracted."

"He said he wouldn't fight me."

"He's a liar."

"He said it'd be cold-blooded murder on my part."

"And he has no respect for tradition," her mother added.

"That's true," she had to admit.

"Rhea. You can't be fooled by his tricks and his charm." Flower paused, then took a deep breath and continued. "I admit he's attractive. And he seems harmless. But he's a Mere, descended from de Meres. He. Will. Kill. You."

"And then one of Violet's kids will kill his kid."

"Yes, or one of your other nieces or nephews, assuming he has already fathered a child, or will in the next couple of years."

For some reason, that caused her a stab of anxiety right in the gut. Chris Mere kissing some bimbo? Touching her, whispering to her, caressing her?

"—be distracted."

"What?"

"You cannot be distracted. This is a trick. On top of everything else, he's probably afraid to face you when you're in *your* prime. So he showed up early and tried the de Mere charm. But it didn't work. Right?"

She said nothing.

"*Right?*"

"Why do we always take people from behind?"

Her father blinked. "What?"

"I was taught to strike from the rear, every chance I could get. Even most of the practice mannequins are facing away from us. How come?"

"Because we need every advantage over a magicks user."

"Magic," she corrected.

"Yes."

"Well. Our family has a rep for cold-blooded murder—"

"Defending the family and the town is not murder!"

"—we always hit from behind—"

"Because we cannot do magic!"

"—and we've been killing his family for centuries. Some of them a lot more helpless than Chris Mere."

"That is our duty!" her father practically screamed, his bald spot turning purple with rage.

"You know what? I think we *are* the bad guys."

"Rhea!" her parents howled in unison.

"No, really. We are. He came in peace—twice—and all you two can do is talk about how it's some cruel trick. Because you'll never trust a Mere."

"True enough," her mother said.

"But I think *I* can."

"Oh, Rhea."

"You guys weren't here. I was beating the shit out of him, and he took it. Not only did he not use magic on me, he didn't use his upper body strength, either. Well, not too much."

"That was not how it appeared when we drove up," her father said sharply.

"You're right. That's not how it looked. Which proves my point: Appearances are deceiving. What if we've had the wrong idea for three centuries?"

"That's—that's—" Her father shook his head. "I would have to give the matter some thought."

"Also, I think I know how to break the curse."

Her mother slumped wearily into one of the kitchen chairs. "This *is* the curse. To kill and be killed, again and again and again. To bury your mothers and your aunts and your sisters and your nieces."

"No. There's a loophole, and you know it."

Her parents were silent. Finally, her father tentatively said, "If he shares his powers with you?"

"That and one other thing."

"What?" her mother asked.

"Never mind. I don't know if I can pull it off. The important thing is to find him."

"*Find* him?"

"Yeah. I have to find him before he turns thirty and I have no idea where he is. Too bad for him I memorized his rental car license plate. It'll be a start."

"Rhea, you cannot do this."

"I'm calling your bluff, Mom. Because I'm *not* going to kill him. If you think killing me will fix that, you've gone over to the dark side for sure. And we're already there, damn it."

"Rhea, you know I—you know I would never hurt you. I-I was angry and I didn't mean—"

"Don't do it, Rhea," Power said quietly, sounding for the first time in a week like the superb trainer and parent she adored, instead of the shrill, easily angered man he had become after Chris showed up. "It's a trick. He'll kill you. Please don't go after him. Stay here and train. Maybe—maybe you can break the curse if you break him."

"You guys. I have to do this my way, because the old way doesn't work. I'm telling you: *I can break the curse.* Isn't that worth the risk? Think about it, Dad. No more training, ever. Not having to flinch every time a stranger shows up in town. Saving Violet's baby! Or Ramen's, or Kane's. Not having to bury me."

Her father couldn't meet her gaze and turned to stare out the north window. Her mother, however, looked hopeful for the first time in a week. "Oh, Rhea, do you really think so?"

Actually, I have no idea if my plan will work, but don't give it another thought. "Absolutely," she lied.

Her father stood with his back to her, still staring out the window. "Then go," he said, "quickly. While there's still time to catch him. Do—do you want me to come with you?"

"I'll come, too," her mother added, though she wasn't a Goodman by blood, of course.

"My, my, look at you two. I'm shocked to my very core. Breaking tradition like that? No chance," she teased.

"Mmm. And Rhea . . ."

"Yeah?"

"If it goes badly—"

"I know, Dad."

"Because it may be an elaborate charade on his part."

"I know, Dad."

"To trick you into lowering your defenses."

"Gotcha."

"Why was he the one on top when we drove up?"

"Uh—gotta go, Dad."

Chapter 9

Call girls—or "soiled doves" as Chris preferred to think of them—had been disappearing in Boston for more than two months. Chris drove yet another rental down to the harbor for a quick look. And a finder spell, of course. Because he had a good idea what was happening. A K'shir demon: The Taker of the Lost. Looks like a man, feeds like a devil, then looks like a man again. Only a magic user could spot it for what it was—a creature so unnatural to this world that it actually made his head hurt.

In fact, it hadn't hurt so badly since the day Rhea had smacked the shit out of him.

Don't think about Rhea.

He tried. He really tried. He'd spent the last two days holed up in his hotel room, determinedly not thinking about Rhea. Trying to become absorbed with the Call Girl Killer.

And in all the not thinking about Rhea, he'd decided what to do: stay away. Don't go looking for her on his thirtieth.

And don't knock anybody up, for the love of God!

He swallowed at the thought. Did he have the courage to end his family line? Could he? *Should* he?

If it kept Rhea and the next Goodman safe, then yes. Absolutely.

Feeling a bit better about his decision, he'd decided to look into the missing soiled doves. All had been lured down to the harbor. Other than that, they had nothing in common, except for the way they died—in great terror and pain.

The police thought wild animals were on the loose, even though no one had reported a pack of wolves gone missing. And Chris couldn't blame them—he'd seen the crime scene photos. A quick show-me spell, a quick forget spell, and he had copies of everything. He had seen. Nothing human could do that to the poor girls. Frankly, he hadn't been able to eat a thing for quite a few hours after looking through the case files.

He had a strong hunch that the cops weren't going to be able to solve this case. Ever. So he would step in, again. In truth, he couldn't wait. All the pent-up anger and frustration at his situation—his and Rhea's, whom he wasn't thinking about—could be poured into his attack.

Go back, the rat in his brain whispered. *Do a spell. Make her come with you to the hotel. Make her take off her clothes and yours and—*

He shoved the thought away. It would reappear in another

half hour or so, much to his disgust. After all the lectures Rhea had endured, it looked like he was the bad guy after all. How she would have liked to hear him say so!

But she would never hear him again. He would see to it. And he would end his line and break the curse. And she could live happily ever after, and so could her niece, the player-to-be-named-later.

He parked near Faneuil Hall and walked toward the harbor. His head hurt more and more with each step—excellent. The Taker of the Lost was planning on feeding tonight. Good. Chris was in a skull-cracking mood.

He stopped near a relatively deserted side street, read a Post-It, then stuffed the note back in his pocket and chanted,

"Taker of the Lost
Show your true face.
Then you'll be bossed
And I'll hit you with mace."

Okay, as far as poems went . . . not so great. Really kind of dreadful. But that was the trick. They didn't *have* to be good poems. They just had to rhyme, even clumsily. What had Rhea said? Get a rhyming dictionary? How had he never thought of that? The girl—woman—was a genius! But more important, why had she given the suggestion? It was kind of out of character for her—for any Goodman—to help a Mere. Frankly, it—

A startled roar from two blocks over smashed up his train of thought; he started to sprint. The demon was likely to lash out at anybody near it; they hated—*hated*—being forced to drop their disguises. He heard a car pull up behind him and slam on the brakes, and was absently grateful not to be creamed by what sounded like a typical Boston driver.

He rounded a corner and ran another block, then checked himself before he could run blindly into the alley. He looked up. And there it was, hanging twelve feet up like a bloated bat—all dark leathery wings, two hearts, and bad smell.

"Don't you want to come down here and kick my ass?" he called up to it, hoping it understood English.

That was when the one behind him slammed into him, shoving him so hard into the wall that he almost lost consciousness.

Two of them? Oh, *great*, as Rhea would say. It certainly explained the number of missing girls . . . he'd assumed it was a ridiculously hungry demon, not that it had a mate. Demons of any kind were not known for teamwork. He should have remembered there was an exception to every rule.

Too bad for him.

He rolled away just as the demon's left foot came down where his head had been, cracking the cobblestones. He felt something warm drip into his eyes and realized he was bleeding from a scalp wound.

It's possible, he mused, that I jumped into this without planning it so well. Anything was better than wondering how things might have been between him and the girl

(woman)

he wasn't thinking about. Even facing an extra demon on a Wednesday night.

He watched with something close to disinterest as the male scuttled down the wall and the female edged closer.

He couldn't think of a thing that rhymed with demon, and he was too woozy to grope for a Post-It and try to read it in the darkness of the alley.

This is it. Heaven, here I come. I'll go to heaven, right?

There was a shhhhk-THUD and another shhhhhk-THUD, and the female, who had been once again getting ready to stomp him, screamed. Chris wiped more blood out of his eyes and saw two arrows sticking out of the female's back.

The demon popped her extra elbow joint loose and was able to reach far enough up her back to yank at them, and then screamed again—in anger as much as pain—when she moved them in her flesh but did not dislodge them.

Shhhhhk-THUD, shhhhhk-THUD, shhhhhk-THUD. More screaming. Now the male was roaring in a rage, but (typical of demons) did not come closer to help his mate, preferring to wait in the shadows to ambush—who?

"You dumb shit," Rhea observed, marching into the alley. She was dressed in super-cool badass black from neck to ankles, and—was that a Kevlar vest?

"It's nice to see you, too, sunshine. Dressed for the occasion, I see. And by the way, ow, my head."

"Taker of the Lost?" she asked, studying the wounded female, who had gone down on her knees and managed to claw out one of the arrows. "To think I thought all those stories my dad told me were fairy tales." Her hand snaked behind her back and she came out with a gun—a really big-ass gun—and emptied six chambers into the female's head. "And for the record, you stinking big bastard, the only one allowed to make him go 'ow' is *me*."

"Stinking big bitch," Chris said helpfully. "This is the female."

Despite their exotic mythology, demons could be killed with conventional weapons: Destroy enough of the brain and it was a fait accompli. So Chris was not surprised to see the female slowly topple forward and lie still.

He *was* surprised to see Rhea squat in front of him and hand him a Wet Nap, which he batted out of her hand. He'd stupidly assumed she had seen the male as well—which was a gross disservice to the girl. Woman. She'd only known about her "duty" for a little over a week, and damned sure didn't spend spare time casting spells on demons. She was a fucking poet!

Those thoughts whirled through his brain in half a second, and he brought his knees up and kicked her as hard as he could, square in the chest. She flew away from him like he'd shot her out of a cannon,

(God, God, don't let her be hurt, please God, I'll owe you one, okay?)

and then two black feet smashed into the spot where Rhea had been crouching.

"Ow," Rhea bitched from eight feet away. Then, "Two of them? In all the stories I heard—"

"Yeah, and all those old stories are always totally truthful."

"Good point," she admitted, climbing to her feet and popping the cylinder on her six, grabbing a speed loader and sliding it home, even as she edged toward the male, who, in a rage, was still stomping on the spot she'd recently occupied.

"Jesus, what are you waiting for? Shoot him! He's alone now, so he's being careful. Which is the only reason he hasn't eaten our heads. Shoot!"

"No. You might be killed in the crossfire."

"Who cares? Shoot the fucker!"

"I care. Freeman, gleeman, semen, seamen, Philemon, cacodemon. Lost, boss, floss, gloss, toss."

The male twisted toward her, hissing, but it had to climb over the body of its mate to get to Rhea, so he had maybe three seconds.

"Taker of the Lost
Begone to where lives a demon
Lest I give you a toss
Then drown you in semen."

"I think I'd rather have my face clawed off than listen to another one of those," Rhea commented as the advancing male suddenly vanished with a loud "pop!" . . . the sound of air rushing into the space it had so recently occupied.

"Shut up. It worked, didn't it?"

"You couldn't think of anything that rhymed with demon, could you?" she asked kindly.

"Shut up," he said, trying not to sulk. They stared at each other from opposite sides of the alley. Then he wondered why he was sulking. She had come! She had (somehow) tracked him down and found him and come armed and—

"Before I embrace you and cry like a little girl, you didn't bring all that stuff and wear all that stuff to kill me, did you?"

"Only if you misbehave." She grimaced, stood, and rubbed the small of her back. "Thank goodness for body armor. You kick *hard*, Mere."

"Chris. And thanks. My fault, by the way. I had no business assuming you knew there were two."

"And I had no business charging into an alley before I effectively deduced the threat level. So we both fucked up. That's why we can't kill each other."

"Really?" he asked, almost afraid to hope.

She bent, found the Wet Nap, skirted the dead female, and handed it back to him. "Really. If we try to kill each other, we'll just screw it up. Excuse me." She leaned against the wall and efficiently threw up.

He climbed to his feet, wiping more blood out of his eyes, then went to her and patted her shoulder while she vomited. "Sorry, sorry," he said, as distressed as he'd ever been. "It's awful, I know. The smell and the—the general unnaturalness of them." He couldn't believe she'd walked into a dark alley to save his ass. "It hurts my brain to look at them."

She coughed, pulled an arm across her mouth, then said, "It hurts my stomach."

"Then why did you come?"

"Oh, I broke into your hotel room and found all the police reports. After I tracked your car rental. It wasn't hard to figure out where you went next—I was right behind you those last few minutes, but you ignored my honking."

"This is Boston," he said, as if that explained everything.

She laughed, a sound that caused his heart rate to double with pure joy. Then her eyes narrowed, and she cut off her laugh and said, "You didn't raise those two, right? You just get rid of them. Right?"

"Rhea. You really have to ask?"

"Sorry. Distrusting you is going to be a tough habit to break."

"Sunshine, you don't even know how tough. So now what? Since you're sure if we turn on each other we'll screw it up. What does that leave? Teaching each other to knit? Taking a judo class at the Y? What?"

She laughed again. "Now we go back to your hotel room and make a baby."

"*What?*"

Chapter 10

"I can't believe this is happening. I just can't believe it."

Rhea actually had to lead Chris through the lobby like a Seeing Eye dog. He was so shocked by her plan, he'd almost gone catatonic.

"I've been spending all this time not thinking about you, and now you want a Mere baby."

"A Goodman-Mere baby."

"I can't believe this is happening," he said again, following her robotically into the elevator.

"Are you all right? You're like kind of . . . out of it."

"I can't believe this is happening."

"It's a good way to break the curse, don't you think?"

"Curse?"

"The *curse*. The one that's been on our families for three hundred some years? *The* curse."

"Oh. That curse."

She pressed the button for his floor. "Are you sure you're okay?"

"Sure as sure can be," he replied absently. "It's just that I fell in love with you and was resigned to never seeing you again, and then you saved me in the alley, and now you want to have sex. I'm feeling a little like a Powerball winner. Also, I think we already broke the curse."

"When you shared your powers with your greatest enemy. And we teamed up and kicked some demonic butt."

"Right, right."

The elevator dinged, and they walked out. She used his key card to pop the door open, and inside they went. The hotel had already done turn-down service.

"Look!" Rhea said. "Chocolates!"

"Help yourself." He was just standing in the middle of the room, like he wasn't exactly sure what to do. Which was problematic.

She gobbled both chocolates, then started taking off her body armor, short-sleeved T-shirt, black leggings, black socks, black running shoes, and white panties.

"What are you doing?" he said, sounding almost—startled?

"Like I'm going to make a baby with body armor on. Don't just stand there. Strip."

"I can't believe this is happening."

"Yes, Chris, I *know*. Strip."

Still moving like his limbs were barely thawed, he started taking off his clothes. Belt, shirt, khakis, socks, shoes (in no particular order, she noted). Simpsons boxer shorts.

"I'll overlook the shorts, but afterward, we really have to talk."

"Did I make fun of your underwear?"

"You were thinking it," she said, taking his hand and leading him to the bed. She was trying not to stare, and failing—miserably. He was just—superb. Long lean limbs, broad shoulders, lightly furred chest, slightly dazed green eyes. And what looked to her like a rather sizeable erection, jutting stiffly upward toward his taut stomach.

"Chris?"

"Mmmm?"

"Do you *want* a baby with me?"

He blinked. "A Goodman-Mere baby? I could care less. *Our* baby? Sure. Oh. You'll have to marry me once you're knocked up. Or maybe next week."

"Good," she whispered in his ear. "Because I want one, too. So get me pregnant. Right now."

Finally, he snapped out of the trance and nearly fell on her as he bore her to the bed, his lips frantic over hers, his tongue probing, his teeth gently nibbling her earlobes, her neck, her cleavage. His hand spread her thighs apart and stroked the tender skin of her inner thighs, which made her shiver beneath him.

He moved lower so he could pull her nipples into his hot, wet mouth, sucking greedily, even gently biting her, and the sensation shot from her breasts to her toes in half a second. And now he was gently stroking the hot throbbing center between her thighs, making her strain against him, making her groan, making her plead.

He needed no such encouragement, just returned his attention to her mouth while spreading her legs a little wider. He broke the kiss to gaze into her eyes, as his hips thrust against hers, hard.

"Ow!"

"What, ow?" he panted.

"I just wasn't quite ready for you."

Sweat stood out on his forehead, and she could see him gritting his teeth as he forced his hips to be still. "Wasn't ready for me?"

"Well. This is kind of my first time."

He gaped at her. "Kind of?"

"Okay. It's my first time."

He started to roll off her, but she grabbed him by the elbows and managed to keep him in place. "A virgin?" he practically yelped. "You're a virgin, and you didn't say anything? And *why* are you a virgin?"

"Why wouldn't I be?" she snapped back. "I've spent my whole life training to kill you, or in school. When the hell would I have time to lose my virginity?"

"Okay, okay, don't get your guns. I was just—surprised. I've never done it with a virgin before." He squinted thoughtfully. "I'm pretty sure."

"Could you not reminisce about other sex partners when you're inside me?"

"Sorry, sorry. Does it still hurt?"

"It's a lot better." A whole lot better. Almost . . . delightful? Yes, delightful, the hot friction between her legs was no longer a burning pain but instead a thrilling amusement park ride, where she went up and up and up. He was thrusting against her with such care she almost wept. And he watched her face every moment.

Again, shuddering all over, he stopped. "Hurts?"

"No." She strained against him, trying to create her own friction. "Oh, no."

"You're . . ." He wiped his thumb on her cheek and showed her the tear. "Crying."

"I'm just so happy. Right this minute is the happiest moment of my whole life."

"What whole life?" he teased, continuing to stroke and surge into her. "Ah, God, Rhea, you really shouldn't say things like 'give me a baby' and 'I'm so happy.' It's hell on my self-control."

"You're doing all—oh!" She felt an all-over tightening and held her breath, and then her orgasm—her first *assisted* orgasm—blew through her like a hurricane, leaving her trembling in his arms.

"Oh, Christ!" Then he was groaning and shuddering against her, and she felt even more warmth between her legs than before.

"Uck. You made me sticky."

His head, which had been resting on her shoulder, jerked up. "Uck? *Uck?* You're hell on the self-esteem, too."

"Not uck for the sex. Uck for immediately after the sex. I mean—yeesh. I'd better clean up."

He clamped down on her arms and squeezed. "Don't you dare move," he growled. "No fair ruining the afterglow."

"Oh, was I wrecking pillow talk?" she teased.

"To put it mildly. You came, right? I was pretty sure you came."

"Oh, yes."

"That's great. Usually I have to go down on—"

"Stop."

"Sorry. Boy," he added cheerfully, grinning at her, "your dad is going to shit when we tell him what we were up to in Beantown."

"Now who's wrecking the afterglow? Why did you bring up my dad? Now I have to call them so they won't worry."

"Be sure to mention your recent deflowering."

"Thanks for the advice."

"And our upcoming wedding."

She shoved and punched and finally kicked him off her. She sat up in bed and didn't bother with the sheet, and could see the admiration in his eyes as he looked her over from head to foot. "I didn't hear a proposal, buster."

"Oh, stop it. You totally fell under my spell, and you know it."

"Ha!"

"What else do you call this?" he asked, gesturing to them both. "But magic?"

"You're a bag of sentimental mush."

"One of us should have a feminine side."

"Shut up," she retorted, then grabbed the phone and started dialing.

Power and Flower made it to Mass General in record time, given rush-hour traffic, and went at once to the maternity ward. Flower was carrying a teddy bear. Power had a gaily wrapped box with a big blue bow on the top.

"Excuse me," he said to the charge nurse. "My daughter, Rhea Goodman Mere? She's having a baby? Can you tell me what—"

A shout interrupted him. "And stay out!" Punctuated by the clatter of an emesis basin slamming into the wall.

"Never mind," Flower said. "We can find her."

They turned and walked down the hall in time to see their son-in-law practically sprint into the hallway. "All right, all *right*!" he yelled back. "Don't come crying to me when you forget how to do your breathing!"

"Chris, darling!" Flower called, hurrying up to him and giving him a hug. "We came as soon as you called."

"Happy birthday, by the way," Power added, handing Chris the gaily wrapped box. "A milestone. You're to be congratulated."

"I found *three* gray hairs on my head this morning, and your daughter—and my daughter—are directly responsible. I'm only thirty-two, and I'm going gray!"

"Well, nobody forced you two to get married and have babies," Flower said gently.

"Quite the opposite," Power muttered.

"And don't worry about Violet Number Two; she's at home with her aunties and uncles."

"Great. If she points a toy gun in my face and pretends to shoot me, I'm holding both of you responsible."

"We can't help it that 'kill the witch' is everyone's favorite childhood game."

"It's not everyone's—"

"What are you doing out there?" Rhea shouted. "Taking a poll? Get your ass in here!"

"Coming, coming!" He gave his in-laws a final, harassed glance before going back through the gates of hell.

"The baby will be your birthday present!" Flower called after him.

"Doubt it," Power said, glancing at his watch. "It's almost midnight."

"Second babies always come faster."

"She's only been in labor for four hours."

"Darling. It's *Rhea*."

"That's true," Power said, and sat down with his wife to wait for another Goodman-Mere baby.

"And . . . it's a boy!"

"Oh, *great*," Rhea groaned. "What was I thinking? I *knew* it hurt like a bastard, and I let you knock me up again anyway."

"Hold on a minute, Mom, we'll get him cleaned up, and then you can hold him." The nurse had to shout over the baby's wails to be heard.

"Listen to the lungs on that kid," Chris said happily. "A chip off the old maternal block."

"Shut up."

"And he's gorgeous."

She perked up, as much as she could in her exhausted state. "He looks okay? I figured he was okay from all the yelling. Violet Number Two did the same thing when she was born."

"Here he is, Mom!"

Rhea stared down in wonder at the tiny, perfect face. The baby was looking up at her with the blue eyes of a fair-skinned newborn, and she wondered if they would go dark like hers, or green like Chris's. She hoped they would be green, because . . .

"Welcome to the world, Christopher Goodman Mere," she said softly, and kissed her baby at the exact moment her husband kissed her on the top of her head.

UNDEAD AND UNPOPULAR

"Terrific . . . Starts off zany and never slows down."
— *ParaNormal Romance*

"Think *Sex and the City* . . . filled with demons and vampires."
— *Publishers Weekly*

"Bubbly fun for fans of the series." — *Booklist*

"Make sure you have enough breath to laugh a long time before you read this . . . This is simply fun, no two ways about it."
— *The Eternal Night*

UNDEAD AND UNRETURNABLE

"Cheerily eerie 'vamp lit' . . . A bawdy, laugh-out-loud treat!"
— *BookPage*

"There is never a dull moment in the life (or death!) of Betsy . . . A winner all the way around!" — *The Road to Romance*

"Plenty of laugh-out-loud moments . . . I can't wait for the next installment of Undead." — *A Romance Review*

UNDEAD AND UNAPPRECIATED

"The best vampire chick lit of the year . . . Davidson's prose zings from wisecrack to wisecrack." — *Detroit Free Press*

"A lighthearted vampire pastiche . . . A treat."
— *Omaha World-Herald*

continued . . .

"MS. DAVIDSON HAS HER OWN BRAND OF WIT AND SHOCKING SURPRISES THAT MAKE HER VAMPIRE SERIES ONE OF A KIND." —*Darque Reviews*

UNDEAD AND UNEMPLOYED

"One of the funniest, most satisfying series to come along lately. If you're fans of Sookie Stackhouse and Anita Blake, don't miss Betsy Taylor. She rocks." —*The Best Reviews*

"I don't care what mood you are in, if you open this book you are practically guaranteed to laugh . . . Top-notch humor and a fascinating perspective of the vampire world."
—*ParaNormal Romance*

UNDEAD AND UNWED

"Delightful, wicked fun!" —Christine Feehan

"Chick lit meets vampire action in this creative, sophisticated, sexy, and wonderfully witty book." —Catherine Spangler

"Hilarious." —*The Best Reviews*

"It is a book for any woman who can understand that being fashionable, looking good, and having great shoes are important . . . even if you're dead." —*LoveVampires*

continued . . .